LIBRARIAN AND THE BEAR
OAK FAST FATED MATES BOOK FIVE

REBEL CARTER

PROLOGUE

Once upon a time, there was a bear cub shifter with a perfect life. She lived in a town, clan, and home she'd always known. The cub grew to be strong and true. Her human form was just as capable as her bear. The shifter brought pride to her clan and worked hard (as bears do) each and every day to bring happiness and strength to their world.

But there were moments, in all the perfection of her carefully ordered life, that the bear felt, oh so very alone. There was an emptiness, an ache, in her heart. The only thing missing from her perfect life was a mate. Every day the bear awoke hopeful, yet went to bed lonely.

But she knew her mate was out there, somewhere, in the big, big world. All she had to do was keep waiting. Keep living her perfect life until they came. And keep believing the One was just around the corner.

Of course, this One would be just as strong and true as she.

One with a heart of gold.

One that was a shifter.

Her Fated Mate.

Yet, her mate was not a shifter and the bear was angry. The perfection of her life broke and shattered by a lesson her fated mate was more than willing to teach.

Her mate was human, but not.

A man between two worlds. The magic of mates in his blood as surely as it was the bear's. But the lesson this bear had yet to learn is that fate rarely cares for perfect.

CHAPTER ONE

Birdie pointed a finger at Emmett. "Where the heck do you think you're skulking off to?"

He frowned. "I'm not skulking."

"You totally are," Birdie took a step closer to the man, her heart squeezing when he mirrored her movement in the opposite direction.

"Stop! Where are you even going? You're my mate." The words should have felt *perfect* coming out of Birdie's mouth. What else would a shifter feel when finding their mate?

Euphoric, blissed out, *utterly at peace.*

Sure, she thought those were probably all viable options when a shifter stumbled on their mate. Especially after waiting so long.

Or at least, they would be if said mate wasn't edging away with wide eyes while shoving a book cart between them.

She frowned watching him. It just had to be a human, didn't it? They were twitchy when it came to shifter ways and Fae magic. If her mate had been a shifter they would have understood. They would have felt the pull, the tenuous feeling coming to life in Birdie that made her ache when she watched Emmett bump into the bookshelves behind him in his scramble to put distance between them.

Why did this have to happen to her?

Why a human?

"You're my mate," she said again, and the words felt sour in her mouth. Heavy and sharp-edged, a knife twisting and sinking into her belly with each and every inch Emmett put between them.

"Where are you going?" Birdie whispered, hands clenching into fists. She wanted to chase after Emmett, to touch him, to bury her face in his neck and feel that spark that just passed between them again.

"Oh no," Rosie murmured, hands covering her mouth as she watched. Birdie ignored her friend and forced herself to stay where she was even while Emmett's head whipped back and forth, searching for an exit route. She couldn't bear seeing the look of sadness and pity in Rosie's eyes. If she did, she might break.

"I have to get out of here," Emmett said and threw out his hands. "Now." He looked anxious, panicked, definitely like he was two seconds away from bolting from the library. Birdie thought he might have if she hadn't been between him and the aisle that led to the door.

"Where?" she asked, voice coming out in a croak. She'd never imagined meeting her mate would go this way. Yes, a human mate was the most challenging to have. They didn't get it the way a shifter, fairy, or even a witch did. Witches were hard, but they understood the magical nature of the world and how the ancient arcane made the rules when it came to things like mates.

Non-magical humans didn't have the same kind of understanding. And from where Birdie was standing, there didn't seem to be a single magical thing about Emmett. A pity really.

"Anywhere!" he exclaimed. "Anywhere that isn't here. Anywhere that isn't with you."

Birdie winced and swallowed hard. She didn't like hearing he needed to get away from her, but she chose to be optimistic. He was human after all.

"You need time. I understand."

"I need more than time. I need space."

Birdie took a step back and nodded. "I can do that," she told him and then took another step back, "I'll give you time."

This would be overwhelming. Luna, it was overwhelming *her* and she was a shifter. She'd been brought up to hope and wish for her mate—and now she'd finally been given her fated mate. There had been no mistaking the silver spark leaping between their fingers when they'd touched. Emmett, the new librarian, was her fated mate. She wished he wasn't looking at her like his back was up against a wall, though.

It's not like she wanted it to go like this either. Why didn't he understand that?

"Space. I need space, I can't do this."

She stopped her backward walking and looked at him. "Can't do what?" she asked.

What the hell was he going on about? Every step she took from him was hurting her. All she wanted to do was run to him and she was forcing herself to do the opposite. In the grand scheme of things a living being could and couldn't do, she was doing a big one.

So what was he going on about with "I can't do this?" Whatever it was, it sent Birdie's stomach plummeting and she braced herself when she saw the look of wild desperation in her mate's eyes. He might not be a shifter, but if he was, his animal would be close to taking his skin.

She raised her hands in the way you might soothe a scared horse and lowered her voice a pitch. "Listen, it's going to be okay. All we have to-"

"*This*. I can't do this," he interrupted her with a swipe of his hand. "I'm not anyone's *mate*," Emmett spluttered. *"I'm a librarian."*

Birdie arched an eyebrow. "What does that have to do with anything? You can be both."

"I'm just-" he broke off, "I'm just saying, this is not what I expected moving here, okay? I thought this was going to be a safe haven for me. Not a place where I'd get saddled with a mate."

The knife Birdie had felt in her chest dug in, cutting her deeper and she blinked away the tears that sprang to her eyes. "Saddled? You think this is what I wanted? A human mate?" She let out a scoff and shook her head. "This is my worst nightmare."

Emmett crossed his arms. "And what's wrong with a human mate?"

"Everything," Birdie told him and threw out her hands. "This is the worst case scenario for me, okay? I don't want this any more than you do. A human mate is the last thing I wanted, buddy."

Now Emmett took a step towards her and it was Birdie's turn to move away from him. The earlier panic she'd seen in her mate vanished. In its place was an intensity that put her on edge. There was a change happening in her mate, but what? And why did he have her adrenaline pumping?

She was the shifter. She was the predator here, so why did this human have her backing up?

"And what kind of mate would you have wanted?" Birdie sucked in a breath when she heard his voice. It was lower, throatier. If he was a shifter the man would have been growling.

She narrowed her eyes at him. She didn't like the posturing of the bears of her clan. She liked it even less when her mate had just gotten done telling her how he didn't want to be 'saddled with her.'

"Anything but a human," she told him, standing her ground when Emmett came closer.

Emmett chuckled. Birdie frowned.

"What's so funny?"

"I'm not human."

Birdie blinked at him and swallowed hard. She rocked back on a foot and shook her head. "What do you mean?" She tapped her nose. "All I'm picking up is human." She sniffed the air and then nodded. "100% average, normal, boring and *mundane-*"

Emmett let loose a sigh and crossed his arms at the tone in Birdie's voice. His mate, for better or worse, sounded unimpressed. Rosie held up her hands and tried to move between the couple.

"Now, now, let's just take down the human bashing verbiage. There's nothing wrong with humans. I'm sort of human, you know?"

"So not," Birdie threw out her hands and went on, ignoring her friend, "magical whatsoever, human." She looked at Rosie when she finished. "It's not bashing if it's true. I didn't say anything hateful."

Emmett crossed his arms over his chest. "You called me boring."

Birdie raised an eyebrow. "You're a librarian," she reminded him.

He scowled at her, handsome face pulled into a frown. "What's that got to do with anything? Librarians are plenty interesting."

"Sure, sure," Birdie muttered and then jabbed a

finger in his direction. "What are you so worked up for, huh? You were ready to high-tail it out of here the second I said you were my mate. What's it matter what I think about humans?"

He lifted his chin, meeting her eyes. "Did you miss the part where I said I wasn't a human?"

Birdie's lips pressed into a thin line. "I don't believe you."

Emmett looked like he was ready to prove her wrong but the great big grandfather clock that lorded over the library chimed. The ominous chimes echoed through the room, signifying the time. 11 o'clock. Birdie pursed her lips and scowled over her shoulder at the massive work of wood and brass. It was merrily bing-bonging along, the loud chimes making it impossible to hear a word Emmett might have spoken, not like it mattered.

The chimes had broken the spell and all at once Emmett backed away from her as quickly as he'd advanced.

"I have to go," he choked out when she looked his way. She knew what that meant. He wanted to get away from her. Her heart squeezed and the sudden weight of what had happened between them settled on her shoulders. Birdie wanted to cry. It was so sad as this was the one thing she'd held dear to her, the mystery and possibility of her mate. The fact that he'd been out there until this morning, an elusive thought. A shifter (she'd hoped) that would be her other half. The slice of her soul that had been missing since she'd first drawn breath, would be returned to her.

She'd be wholehearted.

Made complete, when she found them. The spark between them told her this was super charged magic. The kind that wasn't by accident, but directly decreed by the Fae folk. What had they been thinking when they'd paired her with Emmett, *the Librarian?*

The man wanted nothing to do with her. She didn't care what he said about not being human, he was. And just like so many humans outside of their territory, he was scared of her. She could scent that on him. The apprehension, the need to get away, the anxiety and anguish that came with the knowledge that he was her other half.

No. *No.* This was all wrong. It wasn't supposed to be like this.

Not with her mate.

"Don't worry, I was leaving. You can stay," Birdie whispered when the chimes stopped. Her voice, though, was lost in the jangling echo of it all.

"Birdie, wait!" Rosie started for her friend, but she waved her off. Birdie needed time to think, and for that she needed to be alone. She turned on her heel and stomped out of the room, past the rows of books and the dozing woman by the front door. She pushed the heavy doors open and sprinted out into the sunlight.

She made it three steps before she shifted and then, she just kept running.

CHAPTER TWO

Birdie ran for as long as she could. Her legs burned and her lungs, goddess, her lungs felt like they might burst from how hard she pushed herself. The world passed in a blur. The trees beside her, the sky above her, the rocky ground beneath her paws, all of it blurred into one endless wash of form and color around her. It was rarely like this for Birdie.

When she shifted, she saw the world in hyper focus, it was like someone flipped a high def switch on the real world until it was all magic.

Magic was dangerous.

It belonged to the Fae and to the witches. Shifters were wary of it generally, but Birdie didn't see it that way. She understood that shifters and magic were intertwined. It was impossible to have one without the other.

She might not understand it, but there were plenty

of things she didn't understand. She wasn't afraid of quantum physics, how to fold a fitted sheet, or tax deductions. And she really, really, should be, seeing as she was pretty sure she filed her taxes wrong this year, but whatever.

You live and you learn.

You set up a shitty payment plan and moved on, or at least that was when it came to the small stuff like taxes. That was the human world. It got complicated when it came to her world

The magical world.

The Fae made the shifters, the Fae controlled the magic and all those that used them. There were the witches though, that pushed back against the Fae folk. Which was nice, seeing as they thought they ran things in the supernatural world.

Birdie ran faster. Her bear was smaller than the rest of her clan and instead of a coat of dark brown or one made up of tawny hues, she was silver.

Almost white, but more ash, like moonbeams on an Aspen tree. Some of the other members in her clan thought it beautiful and whispered about the fact that she might be moon-touched, like it was a good thing. Birdie didn't care much for all that talk. It made her feel apart from them. She didn't want that. They were her clan. Her blood. Her way through the world that made sense to her when everything else didn't.

The world so often didn't make sense to her.

She had just never thought it would be that way

when it came to her mate. Not just her mate, but her *Fated Mate*.

Those were different.

The fates had made it that way, designed their world and universe in such harmony that the bonds between Fated Mates just moved through the world in a different way. The magic was weighted more heavily, influence and destiny had their say when it came to Fated Mates. Birdie's father had often grumbled that the Fae Queen had her hooks in Fated Mates.

"They're nothing more than pawns to her. You'll see what I mean one day."

What he said was the sort of thing shifters thought but rarely dared to say out loud. Their gift to shift and their link to the Moon Goddess was made possible through Fae Magic. Stuff older than time, the kind of power that seeped into the world and came back out again when you least expected it. Fae were like that, though.

So were Fated Mates.

Birdie came to a scrabbling stop, claws sinking into the rocky ground as she forced herself to stop running. If she didn't, she'd keep going and that would take her clean out of her clan's territory. She didn't really think she needed to be anywhere but Iron Tooth land right now. Not with how she felt.

She huffed, a big breath coming out of her in a snuffle. She didn't feel right. When she was in her bear form things were easy, all of her worries from the human world melted right off her like water of a duck. Whatever was bothering her family, the clan politics, the fact that she needed to maybe work a double at the bar, or that her car was a touch too old and was constantly giving her check engine light warnings, were all gone in an instant.

It was just her and her bear.

The two of them were easy. She fucking loved being a bear, but right now? Right now it sucked a big one. Her bear growled. It paced and flicked its ears in agitation. It felt like a barely controlled storm that Birdie had to keep forcing back on track. If she didn't, her bear would run its ass right back to town and claim Emmett without a second thought.

Birdie's body shook, a ripple going through her fur before she fell forward onto her hands and knees in the dirt.

"Absolutely not, you nut," she hissed and squeezed her eyes closed. "You are *not* going back there. He doesn't want us." The last two words were hard to get out and she almost bit her tongue as she said them. Birdie said them all the same, though, because they were true. There was freedom in the truth or some shit like that according to human wisdom, wasn't there?

"Fuck," she gritted through her teeth and shivered. A cold wind blew through the trees, the tops of them groaned and swayed under the force of it. She wouldn't normally feel it. Shifters ran hot, especially bears. It was odd that she felt it so acutely, but it had to be something to do with her mate rejecting her.

He didn't reject you. Maybe he's scared.

"He might as well have," she bit out at her thought. She didn't like that she was giving him such leeway, even if it was inside of her head. She needed to get that locked down, because no one just rejected their fated mate. Of course, there were those that needed a little work, like Rosie, but even she'd given Eric a shot once she'd gotten over the shock of it. Sure, he'd needed a little thing like a Courtship Contract to pave the way, but he'd had the chance.

Emmett hadn't even given her that. It'd just been a brush of their fingers and then he'd been putting space between them faster than Birdie could process. It sucked. One second he'd been laughing, so rich and warm that it moved over her like the honeyed topping her mother put on the pastries they made together for a fall treat. She'd been moved, had stepped right into him and wanted more of it, and that's when they'd touched. Just fingertips, before he was shaking his head and trying to escape her.

"I have to get out of here."

Her heart had shattered. Felt like it was breaking into a million stupid little pieces and her mate hadn't cared. He'd only kept taking those quick and careful steps away from her, making the space between them that much bigger by the second.

"Listen, it's going to be okay. All we have to-"

"This. I can't do this," he interrupted her with a swipe of his hand. "I'm not anyone's mate," Emmett spluttered. "I'm a librarian."

She'd tried to be patient. She really had wanted to soothe her mate. She knew humans had a lower threshold for this sort of business. It was easy to understand. They didn't grow up looking forward to a mate. Didn't have that urge hardwired into them like shifters. She could help him see that this would be a good thing. That it was going to be the best thing that ever happened to them.

Humans panicked. It was in their nature. Who was she to hold that over anyone's head? She shifted into a goddamned bear for crying out loud. She could be patient. She might have, but it was a little hard to see the way forward when your mate said they didn't want to be "saddled with a mate" and made it apparent they only wanted to get away from you.

"What the actual fuck, Luna?" she asked, raising her head to look up at the sky. There would be no moon tonight, it wasn't the right time for it, but soon. She knew the moon would show her plotting idiot cratered face soon. She had a fucking bone to pick with the bitch.

"This isn't fair," she said, but there was no one to answer her. Just the howling of the wind through the trees. Birdie rubbed her chest, fingers splayed over her heart and shook her head. "How could you do this to me? It's all I've ever wanted!"

It was true. Living her life in Oak Fast with her family, her clan, the streets she knew well, the forest she loved and grew up in. Those were all things she refused to give up.

She knew it was a long shot to find her mate if she didn't leave Oak Fast. Didn't care to leave her bubble that encompassed Iron Tooth territory and the humans and shifters that fell within the city limits of the little magical town she knew and loved so well, but she was okay with that.

She was fine with it if she could have them, or so she thought.

It's funny what you think you can be okay with when you don't know any better. Now she knew better. Now, Birdie knew what his beautiful face looked like in the early morning light, what it was to hear him laugh, have his voice wash over her.

Goddess, she couldn't do without it. She needed it. Already it was like there was a gaping hole in her where he should be. But she couldn't fix it, because there was no way to fix it. No one told you what to do when your mate didn't want you. It wasn't a fate the elders talked about and now Birdie knew why.

It felt like dying.

Or as close to dying as she knew. She closed her eyes and tried to breathe but every breath she took hurt. It was like a punch to the ribs. Her chest ached, and before she knew it she was crying. Hot tears fell from her eyes and she hated that. Birdie hated crying. She hated it even more right now because it was her mate that had done it to her. This wasn't supposed to happen.

"This isn't fair!" she screamed, the sound ripping from her body so acutely she felt it as surely as a physical blow. "He's supposed to want me," she then whispered. "To love me and-and keep me safe. To have a family with me, join clans with me, make me strong. Not *this*." Her words ended on a croak. With him wanting to be anywhere but with her.

It hurt. Goddess, it didn't just hurt, it *ached*. She pressed the heels of her hands to her eyes and tried to focus on her breathing. She was tired. Her body ached and thinking about how she was going to go forward from this was too much right now for her human self. For that reason she let her bear take her skin again. The transition was easy, the pain of it nothing to the heartache she'd been trying to escape and she sank into her bear's consciousness as quickly as she could.

She went deeper than she ever had before while keeping a firm hand on its urge to track Emmett down. She knew the bear would do it if she didn't keep her close, but by some miracle her bear was content to simply be. It wandered the forest. It snuffled at bugs and grubs, it basked in the moonless night and walked the paths they knew well and liked best.

The cool night air ruffled their fur as branches and twigs crunched underfoot. They even found their favorite fishing spot and pulled a fish out to eat. A nice fat salmon that made her bear hum with happiness. It was enough to keep her sated and on the move through the night. It was only when the dawn began to rise, those first pink and orange hazes of light streaking across the dark sky, that her bear gave her skin back.

Thankfully, it was right at her doorstep in town. She was grateful for the small favor as her bear had once made her walk the entire length of Oak Fast with nothing but the smile on her face. It was still talked about in town and now she kept a few spare sets of clothing around various points in town to stop a repeat performance. When Birdie shifted back and saw her front door, the familiar brown wood of the door that led up a length of stairs to her loft apartment above the seamstress/Pilates combo in town, she knew her bear had pity on her. What had happened to them had sucked. It was worse than worse.

A shifter's nightmare.

It was no small comfort to know that her bear was on her side. She hadn't locked her door when she left yesterday morning so she let herself and only relaxed when the door shut behind her.

Yesterday was just that. *Yesterday*. She would grow from this. She would figure this out. It would be dealt with once and for all, but first?

First, Birdie needed a good long sleep. Rest would put her right back on path with what she needed to do as not only a bear, but a woman. Once she got that, the rest would come.

Of that, Birdie was sure.

CHAPTER THREE

"I think he just needs some time, you know?" Rosie bit her lip and shifted from foot-to-foot as she spoke. Birdie could tell her friend was trying. She was doing her absolute best to keep her from losing her shit over the fact that she'd been rejected, which might have been necessary the day it happened or even the next, but all it took was a couple days rest and a lot of alone time for Birdie to remember exactly who she was.

She was the daughter of Magnus, Beta to the Iron Tooth Clan. She was the daughter of Elodie, the Seer of their clan. She was second choice to none. She was sought after. She'd bagged an Elk her first hunt. She had worked as a peacekeeper and patrolled her territory borders with her kin as diligently as any other clan member.

She was worthy.

Even if she had done none of those things, or had no family to speak of, Birdie would have been worthy of a mate that wanted her. Not a human who couldn't get away from her fast enough.

"It's fine. I promise," Birdie told her friend. She looked over the clipboard in her hand and took stock of the liquor bottles in front of her. She was doing inventory and would need to skip back to look at their kegs, but everything seemed to be in working order. "Hey, has Eric figured out what he wants me to get for the special Fall Festival menu?"

"Yeah, he has, but I mean, that's not important right now, Birdie."

"What do you mean it's not important. Of course it's important. This is the time we get to stick it to the Silver Tails, bunch of overconfident foxes that need an ass kicking. Can't believe a bunch of foxes are trying to take us on with a *cafe*. Who do they even think we are, huh?"

Rosie swallowed and then nodded. She paused like she was playing for time, maybe trying to pick her next words carefully.

"Listen, I just want you to know that I'm here for you if you need to talk about anything."

It was natural for her friend to offer. Even more so since her mate was going to be her Alpha. That made her second in command among their people. Then there was the fact that her friend had been there when Emmett had rejected her. Rosie had a front row seat to

Birdie's little journey through Fated Mates, whether she liked it or not. Birdie lifted her clipboard a little higher and gave Rosie a tense smile. She knew her friend just wanted her to be okay. She knew it down to her soul.

"I'm okay, really," she lied and gave her friend a bright smile. She willed it to reach her eyes, but it didn't quite do the trick if the pinched look Rosie gave her was any indication.

"Cut the shit, Birdie."

Damn. Guess she was easier to read than she realized. There had to be classes or something for that, right?

"It's okay to be hurt, you know?"

Birdie dropped her eyes to the clipboard in her hand. "You rejected Eric. Everything worked out okay."

Rosie let out a soft sigh. "That's because I-well, I mean, yes. It did work out okay. But it's okay to be hurt. I hurt him. I know that now. I knew it the second I accepted the bond, but there are a lot of reasons a human wouldn't want a bond with a shifter. I mean, I didn't really reject him. Not in my heart."

Birdie nodded, but she couldn't stop herself from saying, "He's not a human."

"You said he smelled human though, right?" Rosie asked. Her friend rocked back on her heels and gave her a raised eyebrow.

Birdie bit her lip and nodded. "Yeah, I mean I thought he did. But...he said he wasn't, and that just didn't feel like a lie," she said and then let out a bitter laugh, "but what do I know? I mean, he doesn't even want me."

Rosie winced. "It's not that he doesn't want *you*. I bet that's not true."

"What do you mean?"

"It's a lot for a human. I was a witch and I knew what was happening and it was *still* so much for me to get a grip on so fast. Shifters are different. You've been raised to look for this, but humans? That's not the same, and okay, what if he's not human and that's why he knew what a mate was? I mean, that's good, because it gives a starting point. What if mates mean something different to him than they do to your clan? The Iron Tooths are different. You know that."

Birdie frowned. It wasn't that Rosie was wrong. Her clan *did* view mates as sacred, Fated Mates as a gift, even if her father had his own ideas.

"If he would have just let me explain before saying he couldn't do it. Before he was basically rejecting me..."

Her friend nodded and leaned against the bar top. "Yeah, he could have just given you a second. But remember, I didn't give Eric a second. I just reacted. Maybe he's doing the same thing."

Birdie's fingers tightened on the clipboard and she laughed. It wasn't her true laugh. Her real laugh was bright and bubbly. Unfettered with worry. It was the kind of laugh that made you turn to see who made it.

This laugh?

This laugh was brittle, controlled, it was something that sounded measured.

"I don't care what he's doing," she bit out. It was true. She didn't. At least as much as she could make herself not care. It was hard though. The Fated Mate bond hit shifters differently than it did humans, witches, even the Fae. For them it was there, a pressure they maybe were aware of before they began to truly accept the bond. If they were determined to resist it, worked to pay it no mind or refused to give it room to take root in their heart...well, they could ignore it for a while.

Shifters though?

No such luck. From the beginning the bond was like an ache. An itch that could not be scratched, the way it was when you accidentally walked into a spiderweb and though you could not see it, you still felt the silky grab of the web on your skin. Rejected mates felt like pure frustration.

Rosie frowned. "Birdie, you can talk to me."

Birdie clutched her clipboard to her chest. "I know," she said. Her voice was small, and she gave Rosie a tight smile. It wasn't her friend's fault that it had worked this way for her. She didn't want to take her frustration out on Rosie. She loved Rosie.

"I know," she said, in a gentler voice. "It means so much that you-I mean, that you're here. That you're being supportive."

Rosie sidled closer to the bar. "That's because I

know what it feels like for you. At least, in a way."

"You do?" Birdie asked in surprise. "But Eric was head over heels for you from the second he saw you."

"Take a seat," Rosie said with a jerk of her chin towards the barstools. Birdie didn't know what else to do, so she sat. She watched as Rosie rounded the bar and headed straight for the top shelf liquor bottles. She plucked a particularly rare vintage of whiskey from the top and Birdie let out a low whistle.

"Eric's gonna be pissed," she said, watching as Rosie poured out the alcohol in two tumblers.

Rosie smirked and added another finger of liquor to each glass. "Good." She nudged the tumbler towards Birdie, and for a second she didn't dare take it.

"Oh, come on. What's he gonna do? I gave it to you. Besides, he gets into the good stuff all the time."

Rosie had a point there. If there was any time like the present to taste the finer things it was right now.

"You don't have to tell me twice," she muttered and snagged the glass.

"Cheers." Rosie lifted her glass and took a seat next to Birdie.

"Salud." The friends clinked glasses and drank. The quiet of the bar was serene in moments like this. It was normally bustling, and would be full up to the brim, standing space only, when the Fall Festival was under-way. She heard a peal of laughter outside. It had already started, at least sort of. The townsfolk of Oak Fast were busy setting up the fairgrounds to the East of town, and even more were turning Main Street into a magical space with stalls, food vendors, music and carriage rides. There would be no cars allowed, not in the downtown of Oak Fast while the festival went on this week.

It was nice when it slowed down this way. Visitors came to town in awe of their ability to walk everywhere, the quaint charm of her magical, but sleepy little home shone bright then. It was easy for her to remember why she'd never left Oak Fast. Why she preferred this slice of the world the best, even when she could go anywhere.

It was nice to travel and see, but anywhere and everywhere wasn't home.

There was only one of those. Oak Fast would always be that for her, no matter who came and went, this place would be hers. The burn of the liquor warmed her belly and made her lips go slightly numb. She licked them and leaned against the bar with a sigh.

"I said that I knew what it was like for you, and I do. At least kind of," Rosie started. She twirled her crystal cut tumbler on the bar with a sigh. "I know you all know the story of how Eric pursued me, that he came up with that insane Fae Courtship Contract to get me to date him, but there's more to it than me just being stubborn."

Birdie nodded. "Your family, right?"

Rosie nodded. "Yeah, at least...kind of. They did the damage but the rest of it was on me."

"What do you mean?"

"I mean that I never knew what it was like to have a home, Birdie. Not like you and Eric. Not like your clan, who can't think of any other place they might want to be. I've never lived anywhere like Oak Fast. And I'm not just saying that because my mate is here. This place is different. The magic that runs here is old. It calls to you."

Birdie tilted her head to the side. "What do you mean?"

"I mean Oak Fast literally calls to any being with magic in them. It pulls you here and you don't know why. It feels...intense and confusing but you know you want to try and figure it out, even if it's scary. That's what I was doing when Eric found me." Rosie frowned and looked down at her hands. "I didn't know what to do when he was there. Larger than life and telling me that I was his mate. That we were fated. It felt like I had no choice, and that's why I came here. To try and figure it all out, but then–"

"The pull of the magic made it feel like you couldn't leave," Birdie guessed.

Rosie took another sip of her whiskey and winced. "Yeah, like my feet were in cement shoes. I came here looking for an answer, or a solution, or I don't know, the next level. But I got a mate instead. I didn't fucking know what I was doing."

"That sounds overwhelming."

"It was. I was reckless with my mate bond. I wanted to assert my independence, so I pushed Eric away like an idiot. I almost ran from him even, but it didn't mean that I didn't want him, and I think that maybe that could be what's going on with Emmett. I know it hurts right now because it probably feels like your choice has been taken away."

Birdie gave her a bittersweet smile and leaned her chin against her palm. "How'd you guess that?"

"I know you. You're not this tightly wound normally."

"Is that why you're tryna get me drunk?"

"Buzzed, not drunk."

Birdie snorted and took another healthy swallow of the whiskey. It was strong. Rich and almost honeyed in a way that made it go down a little too easy. She gave a smack of her lips.

"What if I told you I didn't have any lunch? You think I could get drunk by the end of this?"

Rosie barked out a laugh. "I think if you put your mind to it you can do anything."

"Except tempt my mate."

"Oh, Birdie..."

"I know what you're saying, Rosie. That the whole thing is overwhelming and scary. I get that, at least I think I do. I can imagine what it's like being a human and having this come at you, but-" her voice broke off with a croak and she ran her hands through her hair. "But he didn't even give me a chance, Rosie. Not one before he didn't want me. He said he couldn't do it.

That he had to get away from here. That he didn't want to be saddled with me."

"Not you, a mate."

Birdie snorted. "That really doesn't make me feel any better, Rosie."

"Luna, I know. I'm sorry, sweetie."

"Do you know why shifters are so ready for their mate from the start? Why we don't need convincing?"

Rosie shook her head. "No. Eric mentioned something, but he never really went into it."

"Probably because he wanted to look cool."

"Clearly. Tell me."

"Shifters weren't made the way all the other supes are," Birdie told her. "The Fae Queen made us especially. Fae made, artisanal. I gotta tell you it sucks with stuff like this." She went silent for a beat before she continued, "The Fae Queen made it so that we felt the pull immediately. We can't fight it, even if we wanted to. It feels like a part of us has been stolen, a part of our soul." The pull of a mate could cause a shifter to go mad. Why cubs and pups were educated on the matter as early as they could. It wasn't like that for anyone else, though.

The Fae Queen must have been pissed the day she decided to create shifter bonds. That, or she had a sick sense of humor. From the way Birdie heard it, both were probably the case.

She shrugged and looked down at her stomach as if

she might see the missing part of herself she talked about.

"I don't know what it is, but it's like-it's like I was whole and when he didn't want me, he took a part of me with him. I can feel it. I know he's nearby, that he has that piece of me in his pocket, and you know what sucks?"

Rosie stared at her with rounded eyes and shook her head. "No."

"That he doesn't even care," she whispered. "That for all he cares, I'm tossed in that pocket with his spare change, keys, cell phone...whatever the hell humans keep on them. I'm just in there with the rest of the junk and he gets to go right on his merry little way like nothing's wrong. I guess that's the lucky thing about being human." Birdie knew she sounded bitter, but there was no helping it. Not when every time she was alone she heard Emmett's rejection.

"This. I can't do this," he interrupted her with a swipe of his hand. "I'm not anyone's mate."

"I wouldn't say that he doesn't care. He's got to be overwhelmed like I was. Have you, you know, seen him since it happened?" Rosie asked, voice gentle. It had been three whole days, almost four, since it had happened and Birdie had taken care to stay away from the East side of town. That was where the library was.

It was doable now. She'd have to go that way when the Fall Festival was well and truly underway but that bought her a day or so. She'd be fine, really. The town was plenty big enough for them both while she figured out what to do.

She shook her head. "No, I haven't. But I have a plan." She downed the last of the whiskey and set her glass down with a flourish while Rosie groaned.

"What kind of plan?"

"The awesome kind."

"Birdie..."

"Oh, don't be such a spoilsport. I'm just going to see a witch, that's all," she said with a wave of her hand. She sighed, hopped off her stool and then glanced back at where she'd set her clipboard down. "You think I have to finish the liquor stock right now? I'm definitely buzzed, maybe bordering on tipsy and I need to make tracks if I'm gonna get to the witch in time."

"Witch? What do you mean you're going to see a witch? It's never a good idea to go see a witch!"

Birdie flicked a finger at her friend. "But you're a witch and I see you all the time. Explain that."

Rosie groaned and covered her face with her hands. "All I wanted to do was help and now you're charging off to see a witch. Hey! Where are you going?" She cried and leaped off her stool.

"To the witch! You didn't answer me so I guess the liquor stock can wait."

"Luna help me," Rosie whispered. She downed her glass of liquor and ran after Birdie. "Wait for me! If you even think you're going to see a witch without me, you're wrong."

Birdie sighed but waited a beat for Rosie to catch up before she opened the door and headed out into the evening. The air was crisp and cool, the smell of fall was in the air. She could scent woodsmoke and the smell of sugar burning. There had to be someone setting cookies out to cool somewhere nearby. Laughter filled the air as a group of children sprinted by with their arms in the air as they shrieked with glee.

Main Street was undergoing the early stages of its transformation. She could see the skeletons of stalls taking shape, the awnings that would be rolled out and unfurled being carried here and there. Crates of goods rolled by on carts along with stacks of chairs and speakers for the bands that would play in the evenings all week long. Lights were being added to the lamp posts that dotted downtown. These were more like twinkle lights than anything. They had a touch of magic to them which held them in place without supports. The glow they cast was soft and golden and it was one of her favorite things to see. Main Street bathed in that soft lighting that made it seem like a dream come true.

Birdie smiled and leaned back against the wall of the bar while she waited for Rosie to lock up. It was when her friend was fiddling with her keys and muttering that the smile slipped right off Birdie's face and shattered into a million pieces at her feet.

It was her mate.

He wasn't alone. No, even if he was mated it was obvious he had free rein over his will far more than she did. Her mate was with a woman. A woman with bright coppery curls and a smile so bright it made Birdie's chest ache. The way Emmett looked at that woman made the whole of Main Street fade into nothing. It dimmed in comparison to the warmth and light in his eyes for the woman beside him. The way he touched the small of her back as they walked through the chaos of the Fall Festival's beginnings. He didn't try to get away from her.

No, Birdie's strong mate looked like he wanted nothing more than to be exactly where he was. He wasn't overwhelmed the way Rosie had reasoned.

He was fine. He was happy.

The jagged little piece of her soul he carried with him was indeed forgotten. Tucked away and forgotten. She'd been right, but that was to be expected considering the nature of Fated Mates. Birdie was doomed to the particular kind of fate that would give her insight into what Emmett did.

A strangled sound came out of her, it was a sound she didn't recognize. Had never heard herself make a sound like this, not until that moment. It sounded like pain and fear. Loss and longing. It was *sorrow*.

She clapped a hand over her mouth and whirled away when Emmett looked up. She took off at a power walk, hands still pressed to her mouth in case she made the sound again. Luna, she hoped she didn't. She couldn't bear that damn sounding coming out of her again.

"You asshole!" She heard Rosie yell and then there was the slap of Rosie's boots on the pavement before she was beside her. Birdie swallowed hard, trying to keep her tears from overflowing.

"Fuck that guy." Birdie just managed a quick nod as she kept walking. "Where's the witch?" Rosie asked her after a minute.

"Red River," Birdie croaked. She sniffled because it wasn't much use. She'd felt that brush of Emmett's hand on the other woman. It would get worse. She'd know when he touched her, if he kissed her. The longer their bond went, even if he never accepted it, would be a hard thing for her to endure.

"That's not far. I can drive," Rosie offered, steering Birdie towards the side street she parked on. Red River was only a half hour drive south of where they were. It was a town about the size of Oak Fast, the nearest one to them in the area. Which made it handy for what Birdie needed done.

"Thanks."

Rosie wrapped an arm around her friend and gave her a squeeze. "Always."

Birdie heard the truth in her friend's promise, and despite her aching heart she knew there were more ways to love than the way of mates. That even if he had chosen someone else, that she would not live a loveless life.

How could she when she had friends like Rosie?

CHAPTER FOUR

"You really called him an asshole?" Birdie asked. She was sitting in the passenger seat of Rosie's car, where she was already working her way through a pack of Red Vines she'd found in the glove box.

"Damn straight, I did. I can't even," Rosie shook her head and let out as close a sound to a growl that Birdie thought a human could make. "I can't even believe him! He knows he has a mate, and what was that shit about not being all the way human? He knows what a mate is. I know he does, so what? It's not the relationship just the whole-"

"Me thing he doesn't want," Birdie broke in helpfully.

Rosie glared at the road. "He's wrong. You're lovable. Stop thinking what I know you are."

Birdie grinned. "I know I'm lovable. I have a clan,

town and friends that love me and always have. Always will, too. It's not ideal, but I will have a life filled with love, Rosie. I know that. You don't have to be so mad about it. Besides, that's where the witch comes in."

Rosie cast her a sidelong look. "Yeah, about that. What is she going to do to you exactly?"

"Oh, nothing too wild," Birdie said, whipping a Red Vine around the car before she took a bite out of it. "Just snap a bond. That's all."

"Snap a bond?"

"Maybe, more like rip it out? I'm not really sure of the semantics. That's witch stuff."

Rosie hummed but didn't say anything else. She was thinking hard though, if the look on her face was anything to go by.

"Turn up here," Birdie advised her a few minutes later.

"Here? But it's out in the middle of nowhere?"

"We're in Alaska, Rosie. Everywhere is in the middle of nowhere."

"Fair point."

Rosie turned onto the road, which was less road and more a dirt path big enough for a car to travel down, with a frown. The car headlights bounced up and down with each dip and rise in the rutted path. It was truly dark around them. Night had fallen as they drove the half hour out of Oak Fast. Birdie turned her head to look out at the landscape. She could see better than a human, but out here, so far away from any light other than the moon, made it hard for even her to see much.

"It's okay, don't worry," Birdie sighed.

"I'm going to worry. Who is this witch anyways?"

"Her name is Jazzy. She's real old school from what I heard."

"How come I've never heard of her?" Rosie asked. "I try to keep tabs on all the witches around. Eric gets all twitchy when it comes to new covens."

"That's because she's not part of one. She's a loner, I guess. All I know is she's the witch to see about having a mate bond, you know, *fixed*."

"Who told you?"

Birdie fiddled with her car seat and ate another Red Vine. She knew she'd have to tell at some point, so she kept it simple. "There are some old timers in our clan who lost their mates when they were young. Jazzy took care of them."

"Oh."

That was all Rosie said because while she might not be a shifter, she was mated to one. She knew what could happen to a shifter without their mate. Even if you lost them to death, to another, whatever it was. The longing, the need, the bond, it never truly went away. It could drive a shifter moon-touched.

A one-sided bond was no way to live. Birdie was glad there was someone to see to it.

They drove along for another few minutes before the trees widened out into a clearing. At the center of it was a small log cabin. To the side of it they could see a shed and what looked like a worktable and garden. Smoke puffed up merrily from the chimney and vanished into the starry sky above them. They'd hardly parked and Rosie still had her key in the ignition when the door flew open.

A woman with a cloud of white hair poked her head out and pointed a ringed finger at them. "I've been waiting on you, Birdie Salazar!" she hollered out at them as she took a step out onto the porch, hands on her hips. "Now move it. My stories are coming on soon and I wanna get this done!"

"Fucking hell, she's scary," Birdie whispered, but got out of the car all the same. "Hello there, ma'am!"

"Don't ma'am me. Get up these stairs and call me Jazzy. I'm no ma'am."

"Are you sure about this?" Rosie asked her friend as she got out of the car. "How does she even know your name? You called ahead or something?"

"I don't know! She knows because of witch powers? Isn't that something you do?" she asked her friend and then added, "Besides, it's not like I have a choice in any of this. So yes, I'm sure." Birdie replied as they walked up to the cabin.

"You two hens cut your gossiping and get the lead out."

"Yes, ma-" Jazzy narrowed her eyes at Birdie and she bit back the word, "Ah, you got it, Jazzy."

The witch inclined her head. "That's better," she

said, turning away from them with a twirl of paisley skirts. She had a flowy peasant blouse on and no shoes. The whole look seemed more fit for summer than fall in Alaska, but Birdie knew witches didn't abide by the elements or time. They were unto their own. For the most part, they did as they pleased with no concern for the natural order of things. Their magic was not Fae given, but of more arcane stuff, the kind of magic that seeped out of the land, the air, the trees, the very air they breathed.

It was unsettling to some, Birdie guessed, how witches were out of sync with nature when they cared to be. Time had no reign over them. Their power existed through skill and their sheer will to master the arcane.

It was one of the reasons shifters didn't trust them. But seeing as a witch was the only way to combat the Fae magic that pulled her to her Fated Mate, Birdie was inclined to believe it was a load of bullshit.

Who cared if witches weren't beholden to their powers or the cycles of the Moon and Earth like shifters were? They were in control of themselves. Completely and wholly. It was enviable to Birdie.

Rosie gave her a look that said, 'are you even fucking kidding me?' but Birdie powered ahead. She grabbed her friend and pulled her along behind her.

"I know she's a little wild and brassy, but the old timers swear she's the one to see. She's going to fix this."

"I still don't know how I feel about the 'fixing' part," Rosie whispered.

"Stop that damn whispering! I can hear it all!"

Birdie's eyes went wide and she pulled up short. "Shit." She glanced towards the cabin door that was still open. Light poured out of it, illuminating the steps and she shook her head at Rosie. "Just come with me. It'll all work out, you'll see," she said with far more certainty than she truly felt, but there was no other way to go forward.

Her mate didn't want her. He had someone else.

End of story.

If she wanted to hold on to her sanity and any sense of dignity, she was going to have to shifter up and handle this shit. She sucked in a deep breath and bounded up the stairs, Rosie a step behind, and entered the cabin with her head held high. She might be here to get some shady shit done, but she was going to be honest about it.

"What seems to be the problem, Birdie Salazar?" Jazzy asked from where she was sitting in a rocking chair and rolling a cigarette.

"My mate doesn't want me," Birdie replied.

Jazzy eyeballed the paper in her hands and wet the end before she smoothed it out. "How's that bringing you my way?" She wasn't looking at Birdie, but the shifter was under no impression that the witch wasn't watching her. Odd how she was playing possum that way.

"I said he doesn't want me, didn't I?"

The witch looked bored, which was a far cry from the way she'd yelled at Birdie to get her ass in the cabin.

"And you want me to fix it, hmm?" Jazzy lit up her cigarette with a strike of a match and leaned back in her chair to look Birdie over dispassionately. "Pretty thing like you should be able to tempt any shifter with half a brain, honey. Dunno why you need me."

Birdie winced. "He's not a shifter," she explained.

Jazzy inclined her head in sympathy. "Ah, a human. Unfortunate."

Rosie held up a finger where she still stood by the door. "He's not a human. You heard him, Birdie. He said not all the way. He's got to be a mix of something."

Birdie shook her head. "All I picked up was human when I smelled him. I don't care what that librarian says."

"A librarian, huh?" Jazzy puffed her cigarette but now she looked interested. "A halfling then."

"What?"

"*A halfling.*"

"Repeating it isn't going to make me understand it any more," Birdie muttered and Rosie gasped.

"Watch it," her friend said, poking her in the side and giving Jazzy an apologetic smile. Birdie knew why Rosie was acting this way, deferring to the older witch. It was because the power rolling off Jazzy was intense. Birdie could pick it up plain as day and she wasn't as sensitive to it as she knew Rosie was. It was like basking in the sun, but on the hottest day of summer and realizing too late you didn't put any sunscreen on. Like the sun-baked pavement beneath your bare feet when you left your shoes elsewhere. The pain of it was throbbing, the peaks of it so sharp that it made her feel dizzy.

She could only imagine what it felt like to Rosie.

Even still, Birdie gritted her teeth and pretended that everything was fine. She'd done tough stuff before. She'd helped her mother prepare for her second seer quest, she'd babysat the entire McCoullogh skulk of fox shifters without a blink of an eye. Most of all, she'd been pushed away by her mate.

She figured she could do most anything after that. Even if it was being a smart ass to a witch of mind numbing, sunstroke feeling power.

Jazzy's mouth curled in a smile. "I like you, little bear," she said and then wagged her cigarette at her. "I'll help you."

Birdie's eyebrows furrowed. "Because I mouthed off?"

The witch grinned and hopped out of her chair. "Why not? I've helped for less. At least you livened this bullshit night up. It was too quiet."

"Seems about normal for a Thursday."

"For some. Not me, though."

Birdie nodded as if she understood. "Can't say that I'm not happy we don't have to fight the crowds to talk to you. I was sent by the Iron Tooth Clan Elders."

"Yes, Jimmy and Reagan. How are they?"

"Good."

Jazzy nodded and moved towards the counter at the back of the cabin. It was full of jars of herbs, rows and rows lined shelves that poured out across the wide wood counters. Dried flowers and more herbs hung above her head and below her feet was a thick rag rug tied and braided in bright colors. It was a quaint picture.

What you might think of when a grandmother came to mind. Busy cooking away a meal for her family or fussing over late night tea. The contrast had Birdie staring a touch too long at what she was really doing, but when Jazzy looked up at her she forced her eyes away and surveyed the rest of the cabin. It was a small space that smelled of elderberries, amber and woodsmoke and it had the kind of homespun touch that made you want to stay a while, even if you didn't know why. Time didn't exist here. There was a built-in bookshelf that lined half a wall while a bed took up another wall with a wide window above it. Thick blankets and furs covered the bed that just begged to be touched. A fireplace crackled away merrily in one corner with a small dining table for two to the side of it. There were books stacked on one of the chairs, but the other she gestured for Birdie to sit in.

"He rejected you?" she asked, holding a pedestal in one hand and giving Birdie a once over.

"Yes."

"Not really," Rosie whispered.

The witch gave Rosie a look. "This ain't your story

to tell, baby witch." Her friend's mouth dropped open but Jazzy didn't care, she looked back at Birdie. "Tell me the truth. What did it feel like in your heart?"

Instantly, the tears came. The sudden hot pricking of them against her eyelids and the way her skin warmed made her lift her hands to hold back a choked sob.

"Like he tore my heart out. Like he split my soul down the middle," she cried. Birdie squeezed her eyes shut but even then she kept crying. The tears were hot and heavy, the trail of them on her skin making her scrub at her face. "And you know what the fucked up thing is?"

"What?" Jazzy asked. Birdie heard her come closer, heard the grind of a pedestal and then the telltale strike of another match.

"There's another girl."

Jazzy made a growling sound. Her voice came out in a rasp when she said, "But he has a *mate*. What do you mean there's another woman?"

Birdie shrugged. She focused on breathing deep. She still had her eyes closed but she could see the firelight dancing across the backs of her eyelids. Her chest felt tight and she wanted to stop talking, but she didn't.

"I saw them. He said he didn't want a mate. That he," she swallowed past the thick lump in her throat, "that he didn't come to Oak Fast to be saddled with a mate. I can't go on like this, it hasn't even been a week and I can feel the pull. It hurts. It makes me feel like I'm going crazy." She opened her eyes to see the old witch had come closer. She was just to her side now. The light of the fire moved over her, casting her features in a mixture of shadows that gave Jazzy a more sinister look than Birdie had previously seen. She leaned back in her chair and stared up at Jazzy, trying to make sense of it. She wasn't just some kooky old witch living out in the woods and charging cash for spell work to desperate shifters.

She was more. *So much more.* Power pulsed around her in a way that felt like Birdie might be able to reach out and touch it. The only thing she could compare it to was the pull of the full moon. When she was forced to shift, in that moment right before she lost her skin and all control was taken from her at the will of the moon above her.

That's what Jazzy felt like to her.

"You're different from the other witches, aren't you?" she whispered. Birdie didn't know a lot of other witches, just a handful with Rosie included. She knew her friend was a powerful one but Jazzy seemed otherworldly. She was a force.

"Idiot boy," Jazzy grumbled, ignoring her question. "Don't worry. I know what to do. Now, do you want me to set things right?"

Hope bloomed in her chest when Jazzy said that. If she said set it right, did she mean...could she mean to bring him to her? Birdie opened her mouth and then closed it. The question seemed too telling to ask. There was too much need in her to voice.

If she asked it, then the longing she felt for Emmett might send her sprinting out of the cabin and towards him. She might track him down, follow the pull in her chest to him, let his scent bring her right to his doorstep. If she did, what would she do?

Beg, she decided. She'd beg him to have her. The thought turned her stomach sour. She wouldn't beg. He had another. He didn't want her. She might have precious little, but she wouldn't beg him.

"You'll cut the bond out then, right?"

Jazzy inclined her head once and went back to grinding the herbs in her mortar. "'Course I will. There's no undoing it, though," she warned. "Once I do it. You cannot undo it."

A sharp pain, like a heated iron poker stabbed her in the side, the pain of it radiated up her ribs until it clutched at her heart. Birdie cried out, body bowed forward and braced her hands against her knees.

"Fuck!"

"What's wrong with her?" Rosie rushed to her side and looked at Jazzy. "What's happening?"

The witch clucked her tongue. "Her idiot mate is what's wrong. He's touching someone else, I reckon, from the look of her."

Birdie sucked in a ragged breath. "I need it to stop, *please*." It was harder to breathe. Everything was swimming in front of her and she sagged against Rosie to keep upright. "I can't do this. It's going to drive me moon-touched. Make it stop, please."

"It'll cost you four hundred bucks."

Rosie made a strangled sound in her throat. "What the hell? Just help her!"

Birdie put a hand on Rosie's arm and gave it a weak squeeze. "It's okay. I have it." She'd known Jazzy was going to want payment. She'd been warned to bring cash with her and had withdrawn most of her savings on the off chance the witch was on the pricier end. Four hundred was getting off easy when she'd heard the old timers talk about it. Jimmy had made it seem like she would go bankrupt and Reagan said she had paid it installments, but four hundred?

That was a steal.

Another stab of pain in her chest had her wincing. "It's a deal," she huffed and struggled to sit up. Her friend glowered at the witch while Birdie pulled a roll of bills out, all twenties and neatly facing.

"I thought it was going to cost me a lot more according to Reagan, so chill, Rosie."

"That's because Reagan was a little shit when she came by," Jazzy muttered and took the bills with a smile. "But you've been polite. Even called me ma'am. Good manners should be rewarded."

Birdie gave the witch a tight smile. "Thanks. I really..." her voice trailed off and she sighed, sinking back into her seat. "I just want this done, so thank you for even doing it."

"I shouldn't be. You know that, right?"

Birdie bit her lip. "Yeah, I know. Don't mess with fate. The Fae always get their way, blah blah, blah."

"Oh, screw the Fae. Bunch of busybodies. I don't answer to them, but fate? That's an entirely different matter. It gets its way in the end, so I'm going to ask you this. Are you sure you want this? You really want me to take the bond out of you."

She gave Jazzy a nod. "At the root."

Jazzy tucked the bills into her bra and grinned. "Oh, I like you. That idiot boy is going to wish he never fought this. I'll make sure of that."

"What?" Birdie lifted her head to look at Jazzy. Rosie was still holding her up, leaning against her side while a shudder rolled through Birdie's body. It was painful, sweeping over her in heavy waves that narrowed her world down to the witch in front of her. Even with her focus on Jazzy, the words the other woman was speaking came in and out of being. The sound of her voice was like when the radio went out of tune, white noise with only every other word discernible.

"What's happening?"

Jazzy's hands moved over her, one settled right against her chest where the pain of her bond had dug its hooks in. "Shhh, I've got it now. Here it is."

Birdie felt a tug at her chest even though Jazzy hadn't moved a muscle. "Please," she whispered. She had to have it gone. "Just make it stop."

The witch ignored her, eyes on her hand resting

against Birdie's chest. She moved the other close like she was grasping a rope no one could see and hummed with satisfaction a second later.

"This might hurt," she warned Birdie. She looked at her then and there was understanding there. Empathy. "I don't have to do this."

Birdie wavered. She knew why Jazzy was asking her this. It was a big step, one that wasn't done on a whim. A spike of pain, sharp as a bitter winter wind sliced through her chest and she knew then there was no way around it. It didn't matter if Jazzy was right about fate. Birdie knew it. Of course fate would have its way, but Birdie didn't intend to lie down for it.

"Do it," she whispered, the words almost getting stuck in her throat. "Do it now."

Jazzy's fingers pressed against her chest, just a light touch, and then she nodded. "As you wish." She jerked her other hand away like she was yanking the covers off a bed. Jazzy's fingers didn't move, didn't push harder into her than the light touch, but an invisible hand slapped her, hit Birdie square in the chest with such force that she jerked back against her chair. Only Rosie's arms kept her upright. Without her friend's support she would have landed on her ass. As it was, the chair rocked back on its legs and she let out a ragged cry of surprise.

"What the fuck?!" Rosie screamed and held her tighter. "What did you do?"

"Exactly what she wanted from me, baby witch."

"Don't you baby witch me!"

Jazzy snorted at her. "You alright there?" she asked and gave Birdie's chin a gentle tap. Birdie sucked in a lungful of air and shook her head. It felt like she was waking from a deep sleep. There were cobwebs in her brain, like there was nothing but cotton stuffed in her ears, but with every second it got easier. She breathed in another breath and sighed.

"I feel better," she said and Rosie stopped her shouting. "Y-you really did it. You took the bond out of me."

"Of course, I did. My word is bond, you know how those things are."

Birdie gave her a raised eyebrow. "What do you mean?" She didn't understand what the witch was saying. Yes, she'd paid her, but what did she mean about a bond?

"Fae folk can't take back a promise. Business deals count on that. You ought to know that, with how many have been coming out of veil lately. Thinking they can just pop in and out of the planes as they please," Jazzy tutted and rocked back on her heels. "They're insufferable, really."

Birdie's mouth dropped open. "You're Fae?"

"Mostly. That's why I've got a little more *oomph* to me. Sadly that means I'm also bound by Fae rules. It's not so bad really, considering the advantages."

"I've never met a Fae witch," Rosie whispered. She was looking at Jazzy differently now, with a sense of awe that made an awful lot of sense to Birdie considering the power she'd clocked off her.

"Pleased to meet ya. I have to say, I didn't think I'd meet you this way, though," she said to Birdie.

Birdie didn't exactly know what to make of that statement, especially when Jazzy tilted her head to the side and squinted at her and clucked her tongue.

"That child will no doubt be breaking down my door at first light. You should both go so your tracks are long gone by then."

"What?" Birdie whispered. There was something else going on here even if she didn't understand the complexity of it. Something big, though. She was sure of that.

"What do you mean? What child?" Rosie pressed while Birdie tried to clear the cobwebs out of her brain.

Jazzy stepped back. She was already facing away from them, her attention squarely on the counter lined with herbs and tea when she answered them over her shoulder.

"My grandson was your mate. I don't expect he's going to be too happy with what I just did."

CHAPTER FIVE

The ride back to Oak Fast was quiet. Mostly because Birdie couldn't believe her luck. She sat in stunned silence as the dark shapes of the landscape whizzed by. Finally, Rose was the one to break the silence.

"Of all the witches, it was his fucking grandmother?" she hissed and shook her head. "Oh man, this all feels a little too neat."

Birdie snapped out of her stupor then. "What do you mean?"

"You just had your mate bond to your fated mate snapped by his grandma and she knew exactly who you were and that he was your mate before she did it. Not to mention the fact that she knows he's going to be pissed as hell when he finds out exactly what she did. You don't think this stinks of some bigger plan here?"

Birdie squirmed in her seat. Rosie was making a lot of sense when she looked at things that way.

"What bigger plan would there even be? I'm nobody."

Rosie made a sound close to growling and gave her a swat. "You are someone. Don't say that."

Birdie sighed and gave her friend a smile. "I love you very much, but I mean in this scheme. I'm not the one with some half-Fae grandma out in the woods capable of snapping bonds willy nilly. *He is.* Then there's the fact that he didn't want a mate."

"Emmett sounded like he was trying to pretend to be human, or whatever is the opposite of what he is. If Jazzy's any indication it has something to do with the Fae. That could be why you only picked up human when you smelled him."

"You think he's playing hooky from the Fae world?"

"I mean, could be? I thought they didn't let in halflings, but Jazzy's more powerful than any witch I've ever met, which means she's gotta be from a powerful lineage. They might have been making an exception for him."

"But he doesn't want it? He just...he just wants to be a librarian in a small town in Alaska?"

"Maybe? Could be that he came here because of the call of the magic running through Oak Fast and now he's confused at why he's here. That's why he's pushing you away and, well you know." Rosie's voice dropped like someone might overhear them even though they were alone in the car.

They were near town now and she could see street-lights in the near distance. Their warm glow against the night made Birdie remember the scene on Main Street. The one that felt like it had happened days ago even though it was only hours. She rubbed at her chest and sighed. The place where she'd felt the bond, where the sharp pain had flared into being when her mate had been with another woman, was gone. Not forgotten though. It was sore, like she'd taken a punch and ached when she touched it.

"You mean with him rejecting me and then the woman he was with?" She bit her tongue because she couldn't really finish the sentence as she wanted. If she could, she'd say the 'woman he'd been touching.' The pain that had sliced through her in Jazzy's cabin still burned in her. The angry touch of it bruising her even now.

"Kind of. I can see why he might be trying to get away from the supernatural. Fated mates are, of course, one of the biggest pieces of magic you can't escape."

Birdie turned her face to look out the window. The streetlights were around them now, casting them in light and shadow as they drove along the quiet streets of town.

"Mmmhmm."

"But I'm interested in why Jazzy thinks he's going to know what she did, or go to her at first light."

Birdie leaned her forehead against the cool glass of the window. She felt a little like she was hung over. Like her insides had been turned out and she was laid bare to the sensations of the world. Every bump, jostle and roll of the car wheels on the street was wired directly to her too sensitized body and she shivered.

She wrapped her arms tightly around her body and closed her eyes. "That's where the witch is wrong. He's not going to be showing up at her house pissed about anything. She did exactly what he wanted."

The car was slowing. They had to be close to her apartment now.

"Which was?"

"He had a mate he didn't want. Now he doesn't have one. Now he's free to touch whoever he wants without worrying." Birdie's eyes were still closed as she spoke. She pushed herself back from the door and opened her eyes with a rueful smile when Rosie started to protest.

"It's all right, Rosie. Not everyone gets the happy ending or the fated mate. Some of us miss that, but it's okay because we have friends and clan members who love us. I have a home all my own in a town I've lived in all my life. Everyone is good to me here. I'm going to be okay."

They were stopped now and Birdie saw they were in front of her building. The familiar door that led up to the second floor apartment above the small bakery downstairs was there with the little red welcome mat she had and the cheery little brass bear door knocker she'd installed. She smiled and reached for her door handle. At the sight of home Birdie was suddenly so very fucking tired.

"I need to lie down," she told Rosie with a duck of her head. "Thank you for going with me to the witch. I might have chickened out if you hadn't."

"I'm worried though."

"Please don't be. I had to do it."

Rosie's brow furrowed at her words. "I wish it hadn't been this way for you," she whispered finally.

"I know, but sometimes we don't get what we want. The best we can do is nourish what we have and learn to be happy." She hugged her friend then and kissed her cheek before she hopped out of the car and made for her door. Her words were heavy in her mind. She knew they were true, words she needed to learn to truly live by, but they pushed up against where the sore spot of her bond had once been. The ache there proof of what she'd had and lost by choosing herself.

She hesitated in front of her door. Silence would be there waiting for her but it was okay, it was the kind of silence she'd grown used to since leaving her clan's lands to move into Oak Fast proper. It wasn't a lonely silence, or at least she'd never thought of it that way, but now... now things felt different. She opened her door and turned to smile at Rosie with a wave that her friend returned even though she could tell she was worried for her.

Birdie forced her smile to look more genuine and

then ducked inside her apartment. She locked the door with a little snick and even though she wanted to fall back against the door and rest for a beat, she didn't. She forced herself to walk up her stairs, footsteps echoing on the wooden steps until she was at the top. The familiar sight of her apartment greeted her and soothed the ache slightly, but then there was the matter of the sound. The silence that was just...so heavy now.

Why it felt that way she didn't know. It's not like she'd had anything with Emmett. Just their mate bond. But for the bargain price of four hundred bucks that was over now. She shivered and slipped off her leather jacket. She tossed it onto the back of the sofa and headed straight for her bedroom. It was just before midnight, which wasn't late for her. Not with her bear being far more awake in the evenings. She could feel it pushing up against her ribs. It wanted her skin but she couldn't give it to them. She was too tired. Besides, she didn't know what her bear would do. It might not know that they had no mate yet.

The longing and want she'd felt for Emmett might still be alive and well with her bear. Even if she'd had enough strength to shift, she couldn't risk it. Birdie kept walking until she was in her bedroom. She kicked off her shoes and pants and crawled into bed. It was then that she was able to finally, blessedly relax.

Sleep came easier than she might have thought for a shifter just rid of a mate bond.

THE NEXT MORNING EVERYTHING SEEMED NORMAL. Or at least as normal as Birdie Salazar's mornings went. She showered and ate while she read through her emails and messages. She sent a funny meme to Rosie. Fired off a few promises to join her clan's dinner that week, and even swore to participate in the date auction that kicked off the Fall Festival's festivities. She knew she was going to regret it, but there was no denying the good money it brought in, especially with the tourists.

A little mead went straight to their heads, paired with the promise of going on a date with a shifter. Not everyone who offered themselves up was a shifter, but the amount was more than half given the founding families predilection for being of the shifter community. It was an easy way to give back and besides, she knew she could use the good charity of her taking a tourist out on a date to get out of a lot of clan goings ons for the next month if she chose. She loved them, she really did, but it was difficult when your father was the Beta and your mother the seer for your clan. It meant a packed social calendar with little time to do as you pleased.

Birdie was big on the doing as she pleased. It was one of the reasons she worked at Wildin' Waites. Her parents tolerated it since Eric was of good stock and standing in their clan. He would be Alpha one day, which meant working for him was a plus. She wasn't sure if they would be so keen on it if it were anyone else though. She dressed and got ready for work. No doubt she'd be walking into a whirlwind of activity at the bar with the way Rosie was pushing for the small plates dinner menu. She winced thinking of the menu and how she still had to hand out half a box of them but tried to force herself to think of anything else given what had happened the last time she'd been handing them out.

She didn't want to think about that, or her once mate. It was over and done. She'd walk the town and do her duty to spread the menus to every last soul she crossed, but she didn't want to think about Emmett. Her fingers twitched and she rubbed at her chest, her fingers pressing to the sore spot lightly. She was happy that at least it wasn't so raw.

It was healing, even if she carried the hurt. She probably always would, even if she wasn't pulled to him anymore. That had been a blessing to discover. She'd awoken that morning with ease. Her mind didn't automatically turn to her mate, or the fact that he didn't want her. Instead she'd thought about breakfast burritos and that she might like a caramel latte to get her through her day.

If she were smart she'd get a large with an extra shot to keep up with Rosie. The woman was insatiable in her bid to make Wildin' Waites dinner the talk of the festival. Birdie snagged her purse and jacket and headed for the front door. She was thinking about whether she should get whipped cream on her latte or not, or if maybe she might be able to convince the kids over at the hardware store to finish giving out the menus so she could sneak over to Walker's Books, when she opened the door. The crisp autumn air hit her and she smiled, taking in a deep breath. She had the whole morning stretching out in front of her, a whole day to be with the people she cared about and the promise of seeing her clan later.

It was going to be a good day, she could feel it. Birdie stepped out onto the sidewalk and closed her door. She adjusted her bag over her shoulder, feet walking in the direction of the coffee shop and was digging around in her phone to text her order ahead to her friend Alice that worked there when a voice sounded.

"Why aren't you locking your door?"

She jumped, because she knew that voice, except not the way that it was now. The last time she'd heard that voice it had been slightly panicked, there had been no shortage of frustration he'd put into his words then. That voice had wanted nothing to do with her and hadn't shied away from explaining that fact to her.

She turned to look over shoulder and saw Emmett. He was close to her building, as if he'd been leaning against it before he'd spoken. His arms were crossed over his chest, which only made Birdie's eyes drop to said chest. It was as fine a specimen as she had ever seen. She swallowed hard and forced her eyes away from his chest, or his thick biceps, when he took a step towards hers.

It was then she saw that Emmett looked tired. The shadows under his eyes and the 5 o'clock shadow he was sporting gave Birdie the impression that he hadn't really slept much at all. She could see weariness in his face, but his hair was pulled back in a hasty bun, and he was most certainly wearing the clothes she'd last seen him in, albeit far more wrinkled. It all just added to the whole sleep deprived vibe he was giving her.

"What?"

His gray eyes flicked to her front door. "You didn't lock your front door."

She shrugged. "It's Oak Fast."

"What's that mean?"

"I never lock it."

Emmett's eyes narrowed and his mouth went tight. "That isn't safe."

Birdie took a step back from him and swallowed. She was glad to see that other than getting distracted by his chest and his arms, she was standing strong and feeling fine. Jazzy really had ripped the damn thing out of her. She was safe. She smiled when she realized that and her fingers came up to press at the spot the bond had been. That was fine too. Like pushing on a bruise, but so much better than what she had been living with.

She was saved. Stopped from going moon-touched and all that, she wouldn't lose her mind or go feral. She let out a shaky laugh. Best four hundred bucks she'd ever spent.

"Why are you laughing? You're leaving yourself open to anyone that might want to come into your apartment. That isn't safe, Birdie. I won't have it." Emmett's voice dropped as he said those last few words and Birdie stopped her laughing. She might be grateful as hell to what Jazzy had done for her, but where did this idiot get off talking to her like that?

"What the hell? What are you talking about?"

He rolled his shoulders and came towards her, but each step he took toward her, Birdie took one of her own so the space between them never shrank.

"I need to talk to you," he said.

Birdie shook her head. "There's nothing to talk about. I'm not going to have you telling me what to do because no one is going to come into my apartment. It's Oak Fast." She turned her back on him. It was a shifter move. She showed her back because she wasn't concerned in the slightest what the man, or halfling, or whatever he was, had to say on anything that she was doing. Thankfully his grandmother's magic had held.

There was no bond to make her miss him, or long for him, or to feel like shit when he touched someone else. She was entirely free to do as she pleased. Freedom was a heady thing, so she turned her back on her once mate and set off at a jaunt towards the coffee shop. She should definitely get the whipped cream on her latte, she decided.

"Birdie, wait!" Emmett called out to her, but Birdie didn't much feel like stopping. Why should she? He was no one to her now. Just the way he'd wanted it before.

"Goddammit. Just wait, Birdie. Talk to me, please." Emmett was at her side now. She glanced up at him to see that he was looking at her like she had the answers of life and death in her hands. That he had to hear her speak. It reminded her of how she'd felt when she'd first seen him. She knew there were plenty of shifters that believed in giving just as good as you got but for her all her salt, she wasn't one of them.

She sighed and shook her head. "What is it?"

"Why did you do it?"

"Do what?" she asked. She knew it was silly to play dumb but she didn't really feel like giving up Jazzy just yet. Plus there was the fact that she didn't *want* to go over her decision with Emmett. Not even in retrospect. She'd done what she had to because of the decision *he'd* made. And it was a decision that had ripped her apart and left her heart a mess with no one but her to pick up the pieces.

No. Emmett could mind his own as far as Birdie was concerned.

"You know what you did. What you took from me."

That made Birdie stop and give him a once over. She held out her hand and pointed a finger at him. "What *I* took from *you?* Are you serious right now or am I trapped in backwards day?"

"Yes, what you took from me," Emmett said again before he cleared his throat and stepped back from her. "What you took from us."

"I didn't take shit from us. You did, the second you rejected me."

"I didn't reject you. I said I need space and–"

"You said you couldn't 'do this,'" she said with air quotes and then kept walking, though she didn't stop talking. "That you didn't want to be *saddled* with a mate. That you didn't come here for this. That you had to *get away from me.* Don't try and pretty it up now, Emmett, just because I did what needed doing."

"I felt it the second you did it," he said from behind her. His voice broke slightly. "It was like getting stabbed in the heart."

She stopped walking then but didn't look at him. Instead, she kept her eyes ahead of her. She could see the sun was bright and shining, leaves danced across the street as a wind blew them along and the shops were slowly opening up around them.

"That sounds like it hurt," she said.

"Like my soul was being split. Birdie, you–"

"Yeah, you know what else feels like your soul is being split?" she asked and looked at him over her shoulder. He was just a few feet back, his eyes on her face, hands up at his sides, but he said nothing. He was waiting for her to speak. She knew it as surely as she knew her own name. Emmett would stand there for as long as needed until she spoke, but Birdie had never been one to draw things out, so she spoke.

"Your mate touching someone else. I knew it the second you touched her," she told him. He winced at the word *her*. He looked like he might say something but Birdie didn't stop speaking. She raised a hand to press against the tender place where their mate bond had once been. "Right here. I felt it here and I'm not sorry I got Jazzy to rip it out of me, so why are you standing here with me? Go back to her."

Emmett's face went hard. She watched the softness go right out of his eyes as they shuttered to her. "She had no right to do what she did."

"She did it because I could hardly stand the pain of you touching someone else," Birdie bit out and then shook her head. "She said you'd regret it. I didn't think it would be this quick, though."

He came forward, long legs eating up the space between them. Birdie backed up and the heel of her boot caught the corner of the pavement. As a shifter she was normally more graceful than this, but it was hard with the conversation she was having. Just because she didn't feel the pull to Emmett, didn't have the connection of a mate bond demanding that she go to him, didn't mean that she wasn't affected by the enormity of everything.

Last night she'd been writhing in pain from her mate touching someone else. She'd visited a Fae witch on a hunch. Now she was free. It was enough to turn a shifter on their head. As such she wobbled and went to the side trying to catch herself but Emmett reached out to steady her. She was grateful she had the long sleeves of her leather jacket between them, but it still didn't stop her from observing just how strong and big Emmett's hands were. She could feel the warmth of his touch even through her jacket.

He pulled her upright, brought her close to him and Birdie didn't miss the way his breath caught when her hands landed on his chest.

"You and me," he began but she pushed back from him.

She tipped her head back to look up at him. "There is no you and me. It's done. You'd know that if you talked to Jazzy."

"You mean my grandmother," he bit out as his handsome face went stony again, "my grandmother had no right to interfere. She knew what she was costing me. What it would do to *us*." His hands came up to cover hers and he squeezed them with that last word.

Us.

It was clear from the way he was speaking that the *us* was Birdie and him. The pair of them. She bit her lip and swallowed hard. Even without the bond, the way he was looking at her was a heady thing. Like she was the beginning and ending of everything. Luna, what she would have given to have him look at her like this less than twelve hours ago. She would have given up anything, would have tried to be anything, say anything, for just a slice of this.

She shook her head slowly and backed away from him. "There is no us, Emmett. You wanted to be human and now you can be. Or, I mean, I don't know," She stopped and drew a circle around him in the air with her hands, "you can be whatever it is that you want to be. Part Fae, or human, but you got your wish. You have no mate. I thought you'd be happy. You're free now to touch whoever you want."

She wished she didn't sound so bitter but it was impossible. All her life she'd been raised to anticipate her fated mate. That once she found hers life would become better. That it would bloom with possibilities while they navigated life together. Knit their days together until it was one seamless tapestry all their own. Even without the bond, the memory of what it had felt like the night before, seeing him with someone else, seeing Emmett look at another woman with such warmth in his eyes...that had hurt like a bitch. She wouldn't deny that.

She raised her eyes to his and took another step away from him when she saw that, even though he was here on her doorstep the morning after it all, he wasn't looking at *her* with that softness.

He was mad.

She knew that from the way his eyes were narrowed. His body was tense like a coiled spring that seemed fit to snap at any second. If she really paid attention she could scent the smell of magic. Burnt and acrid. Arcane in a way that made shifters twitchy.

He was pissed.

"You're mine."

As much as she shouldn't want it, a thrill shot right through her at his words. She shook her head and put on a brave face.

"The hell I am. You didn't want me before and guess what? Now, I don't want you." She winced at how childish that last part sounded, but it was true. She wasn't normally like this when things went sideways but she guessed mates had that kind of effect, even in the not having them.

She cleared her throat and tried again. "I mean, we aren't mates anymore. I can't be yours, or-or whatever. It's over. I fixed it."

"It was perfect the way it was. There was nothing to fix. Now there is. Now we have a problem," he said, voice bordering on a growl.

That was new. Since when did librarians growl?

For all Emmett's insistence that he was a librarian, he looked nothing like it now. Or at least, not any librarian Birdie had ever seen. There was a touch of wildness to him that hadn't been there before. She swore she saw a light coming from him, a blueish sort of glow that made her do a double take. There was even the tell-tale prickle of magic on the air, that almost metallic scent that made shifters freeze when it came their way.

It was Fae magic to be sure. Whatever part of Emmett that was Fae in nature was awake now, pushing at the surface and Birdie couldn't help but back pedal away from him. She was no match for a Fae. It didn't matter how mad she was, or how much of a halfling he was. Emmett was putting off the same scary intense vibe Jazzy had been before she'd ripped the bond out.

Crap. Could he put it back? Was that a thing?

His jaw was clenched and there was a steely glare on his face that pinned Birdie in place. The couple stared at one another and she did her best to let her bear show itself. It wasn't normally aggressive but she was just as pissed as Birdie had been at his rejection so she came to the forefront.

A growl rumbled low in her chest and it was enough to keep Emmett a safe distance away from her. His gray eyes flashed silver and Birdie knew hers colored in a similar way with her bear pushing for her skin. Emmett moved, the blue light sliding over his hands, slowly up his arms, as he did. His magic charged the air as he moved. He wasn't the same as when she'd seen him the night before with the other woman.

That gentleness and affection was missing so much that she wished she knew why he was even here. He looked angry at her. Why would he want her? And how had this gotten even worse? She'd gone from having a mate that didn't want her to a pissed off Fae on her ass and it wasn't even eight am yet.

"Do us both a favor and go to her. We're done here."

She turned on her heel, determined to put as much distance as she could between herself and Emmett, but she only made it a step before he called out to her.

"There is no one else for me. It's you," he gritted out at her. And even though his words lacked gentleness and warmth, there was a fierceness to them that called out to her. So much so that she had to reach out and rub the place the bond had been, her fingers pressing to the sore spot of skin to assure herself it wasn't there.

She let out a sigh of relief when she felt nothing for him. She didn't miss how Emmett's eyes tracked the movement and he took a step closer to her. Birdie lifted her chin and met his eyes in a challenge. She willed him to stay where he was. Of course she was affected by his little declaration. Any hot blooded woman would be, with a man that looked like Emmett. He was gorgeous. Even in his unkempt state, his hair shone under the morning light, strands of it falling over his forehead and into his gray eyes.

She looked away from him. They were words. Nothing more. Even if the words were the words she had wanted to hear and if she were honest, wanted to hear now. Even without the bond, pride was a hell of a thing. To be rejected from the start still smarted when she thought about it. She hoped she'd think of it less as the days went on.

"That's not what I saw," she replied as she turned away from him.

"I'm going to win you, Birdie Salazar. I'll prove myself worthy of you, just you wait and see."

She stumbled again, but this time kept her feet. She whirled around, prepared to give Emmett a piece of her mind but when she did she saw there was no one on the street anymore. It was just her and the rustling of leaves as they blew down the street.

She shook her head. "Damn Fae."

CHAPTER SIX

"What the hell do you mean he was waiting for you?"

Birdie finished tying off the bow she'd been working on and tilted her head to the side before she gave it a nod. It was a crimson and gold satin bow and the final piece of flair she was adding to the wreath meant to hang over the front door of Wildin' Waites. She picked up the wreath, a massive affair of at least three feet in width, and began to march towards the front door.

"Bring me that ladder over this way will ya?" she called out to Rosie as she walked. She couldn't see all that much with how big the wreath was and damn, she really went to town with the pine cones, hadn't she? There were two sticking her in the chest, which served her right for putting them there in the first place. A bell jingled when she walked right into the wall beside the door and she heard a picture frame clatter to the ground.

"Shit," she whispered and leaned to the side to see it was a framed photo of her Great-Uncle Jean and his prize winning horse. "Sorry, Unc," she murmured and toed the frame to the side.

Rosie huffed over with the ladder and set it up beside her. "I got your ladder now, answer the question."

"You're worse than Eric."

"I heard that," Eric muttered from where he was polishing the bar to a high shine. There was a clatter in the kitchen and they all heard the sound of cursing which had him sighing before he tossed the towel he was using over his shoulder and pointed a finger at Birdie. "Answer Rosie's questions, but recap it when I get back."

"Hey, when you'd turn into such a nosy bear?" Birdie called after him.

"When you decided to visit a Fae witch!" he shouted back as he disappeared into the kitchen.

"She did *what*?" A chorus of voices from the kitchen staff asked and Birdie grit her teeth.

"A woman can't get a second of peace and privacy can she?"

"Not when she's an Oak Fast local."

Birdie sighed. Her friend had her there. "I only did what anyone else in my situation would have done, you know?"

"Of course you did, but that doesn't mean they

aren't going to be curious." Rosie glanced over her shoulder and made a *shooing* motion when a head popped out to try and eavesdrop. "Give us some privacy, Rene!"

"Oh fine," the old cook spluttered and vanished back into the kitchen.

"Listen, it's not that interesting," Birdie sighed and stepped onto the ladder. "I came down this morning and there he was, getting on to me about not locking my door or whatever. We had it out and now I'm here."

Rosie held the ladder and hummed. "He's worried about your safety then. That's good."

"No, it's not good. In what world is it good that he's worried about my safety? And, can I ask, from what? It's Oak Fast! It's safe here."

"Well, not really. Not since those ferals got turned loose in the hills. You know that."

Birdie paused where she was. There had been reports about the ferals, but they hadn't seemed to cause much trouble. At least, she hadn't thought so...but maybe Rosie was right. It was hard to expect peace and civility from a pack of wolves turned human. Though, from what she'd heard, they deserved it with the trouble they'd been causing the local packs and the Fae Queen.

You didn't mess with the Fae. It was one of the first lessons cubs learned in life. Under no circumstances did you disturb the Fae folk. Though...hadn't that been what she'd done? Especially when she'd given her mate her back and left him talking?

"I'm going to win you, Birdie Salazar. I'll prove myself worthy of you, just you wait and see."

Her fingers flexed on the wreath and she forced her eyes back to the wall in front of her. Eric had already put up a good hook for them to use so at least she didn't need to worry about that.

"They're human now. It's not like they can hurt me," she said as she leaned forward to place the wreath in its place.

"It's still best to lock your door. He's right. Stop leaving it unlocked."

"What if I lose my keys? And then what? Everyone will cluck at me about that."

Rosie made a disgruntled sound. "Stop losing your keys then."

Birdie laughed as she climbed down off the ladder. "You know how I am. That's not going to happen. Some of us just don't have the ability to have things appear where we like them." She was referring to her friend's magical abilities. Being a witch seemed neat sometimes when it came to keeping things in line and orderly. Rosie swore she didn't use it for that because of the way it smelled to Eric, but Birdie thought he was nuts. If she had the ability to go Disney princess on her laundry and dishes, she'd totally do it, smell or no smell.

But thinking on that smell...

"Hey, you said Eric doesn't like it when you use magic a ton at your place, right?" Birdie asked as she came down the ladder.

Rosie nodded. "Yeah, says it smells like an electrical fire, or whatever. I mostly just try and keep it out of the bedroom because I'm not going to stop using magic on account of his shifter nose."

"I smelled Emmett today."

Rosie pulled a face and Birdie went on to clarify. "Like, not him, or maybe it was him? It smelled like that, the electrically copper sort of smell I think about when magic is around. Like pennies."

"Why did you smell his magic?"

Birdie rubbed the back of her neck and thought. "Maybe it wasn't his magic. Maybe it was him? I mean, it definitely had something to do with his magic, because the guy was lit up like a glow stick and on Main Street of all places!"

Rosie's eyes went wide. "What are you even talking about?"

"He may or may not have started to go Fae on me."

"*What*?!" Rosie shrieked.

"It wasn't a lot of Fae, just like *a little Fae,* so chill. Like this much Fae," Birdie said and held up her thumb and pointer finger scrunched together to show her meaning.

"There's no such thing as a *little* Fae. What are you? Moon-touched?"

Birdie shrugged. "Could be. I went to a witch to get my bond yanked out so, jury is still out on that. Back to the smell. I mean it was faint but...but it was there when he was close to me. I didn't smell it back in the library but things were sort of, you know."

Rosie dipped her head in sympathy. "Yeah, that sucked."

"Maybe he just smells like that to me when he's going Fae crazy. It smelled the way Jazzy's did but just less." Birdie thought back on what she had scented at the witch's cabin. There had been the usual herbs and general earthiness she associated with the outdoors, but that metallic bite to the air had been there too. Emmett had smelled like that. Not to mention he had vanished awfully fast.

"What did he say?" Rosie asked.

Birdie blinked. "Huh?"

Rosie threw her hands out at her sides. "What did your mate say? I'm dying here."

"He's not my mate, I thought we went over this. Paid four hundred big ones to lose that," Birdie reminded her friend. She picked up the ladder and headed for the supply room where they kept everything. The bar was sparkling and decorated within an inch of their lives. They'd be opening up in an hour or so for the first day of dinner, but she wouldn't be around for it. She had to get to the date auction, which meant she needed to get this ladder packed away and deal with her hair and make up. She'd never hear the end of it from her mother if she showed up looking bedraggled.

"Birdie, come on. You know what I mean. Besides, fate has a way of getting its way. Even Jazzy said that, and she wasn't wrong about him being pissed about it now was she?"

Birdie paused where she was. "Well, yes," she said, opening the door to the supply closet and flicking on the light.

"So what did he say?" Rosie asked while Birdie headed into the closet to put the ladder away.

"That," she cleared her throat, "just the usual," she said because she didn't want to really get into what Emmett had said. If she did, she knew Rosie wouldn't let her live it down. She put the ladder away in its place and hustled out of the closet. She had to get dressed and down to town square before she was late.

"I've got to go get ready for the auction but I'll be back with my date."

"*Birdie...*" Rosie crossed her arms. There was no getting out of this. Birdie bet her friend was going to plant herself in front of the door, or worse, follow her to her apartment and bug her about what that idiot Emmett had said. She was so mad at him. Why had he made it like this? The audacity of him to show up at her apartment acting like he was worried about whether or not she locked her door, and saying he would win her?

She didn't know if she was more pissed about that or him saying she'd taken something from him. From them. He'd been intense that morning, but what if... what if he was waiting for her again? She couldn't exactly afford to test that, given she could see Rosie was gearing up for a fight about this.

If she followed her to her apartment and he was there it would be a scene. She knew it. It'd definitely cut into her time to get ready for the auction, that was for sure. Best to give the witch what she wanted to know and make sure she was on time.

She sighed and bumped the closet door closed with her hip. "Oh, fine. He said he'd win me eventually."

Rosie's mouth dropped open. "What the heck? Why didn't you lead with that?! I ought to throw you back in that closet for that."

Birdie made a face. "Listen, you can't just take me prisoner. I have to go to the auction or my mom will have a fit. Do you really want to listen to her get on me, and *you*, because you would be my captor, about me not making it to the auction on time? Especially when you know the Stronghearts are going to be *alllll* over it. If we lose to them in fundraising they're going to be insufferable. I think I only like Cash's mate out of all of them, and she's not even a shifter. She's a witch."

"What's wrong with witches?" Rosie asked and crossed her arms.

"Nothing. You know I love witches. Look at me and you! Peas in a cute little pod, and Jazzy? Top notch witch in my book."

"Jazzy, yeah, let's talk about that. So your mate–"

"Ex-mate," Birdie corrected. She snagged her leather jacket and pulled it on as she headed for the door, but Rosie didn't seem the least bit deterred.

"Is her grandson and she yanks that mate bond out

of you, and the next morning he's at your front door saying he's going to win you?"

Birdie nodded. "Yeah, that's the spark notes version of it," she said. She didn't really want to get into what he had said about what his grandmother's actions had done.

"She knew what she was costing me. What it would do to us."

It was such a strange thought. *Us.* Emmett used it so casually she could tell that he had been thinking about it for some time. No doubt from the moment he knew what his grandmother had done. That made her curious. What was it that it had cost him? What would it do to them?

She bit her lip, but Rosie stomped up to her and broke her out of her thoughts. "There's more to it. I know it."

"Not much to tell really."

"Liar."

"Oh all right, I'll tell you one more thing."

Rosie rubbed her hands. "Give it to me."

Birdie couldn't help the small smile she gave her friend as she walked to the door. "I did tell him to go back to her. That I didn't really care how upset he was. Because I didn't want him anymore."

Her friend's mouth fell open at words. "I really wish I'd been there to see that. Good. He was such an asshole."

Birdie snorted. "Yeah, showing up today trying to

boss me about locking my door and telling me that I'm his. What the shit is that?"

Rosie threw up her hands. "What do you mean 'you're his?'"

"What the hell are you two going on about out here?" Eric asked as he strode back into the bar from the kitchen. "I can hear it in the back. Can't get the staff to do shit because they want to know the latest mate drama with you," he said, flicking a finger at Birdie.

She groaned and shook her head. "That's it. I'm leaving. Everyone is too damn nosy. If you need me, I'll be at the date auction tonight and don't worry, I'll swing by to make sure they spend their cash here."

Eric grunted in agreement while Rosie made to run after her, intent on more information. Thankfully Eric did her a solid and caught his mate around the waist before she could get far.

"See you back here soon then!" he called out to her. Birdie waved her thanks and hurried out of the bar and towards her apartment before Rosie could get away from Eric. The bear was strong and the future Alpha of her clan but that didn't mean he was going to be able to hold his mate forever.

She made it to her apartment in record time. Though the second her door came into sight she hesitated. The memory of Emmett waiting for her that morning flooded back in an instant and she swallowed hard. Her steps slowed as she approached it and glanced around her to see if he was anywhere nearby but there was no one.

"Of course there's no one. Get your ass upstairs or you're going to be late," she grumbled at herself. She didn't much like that she was looking for Emmett or thinking about him as much as she had today. Wasn't taking the bond out supposed to end that? Why was she thinking more of him now than she had in the days following his rejection of her?

Maybe Jazzy's magic hadn't worked all the way and that was why she thought of him and blushed. Maybe why, when she thought about the way his magic smelled, it didn't have such a horrible metallic tinge, but made her think of a freshly blown out candle and a hint of musk. Amber, maybe? It was sort of pleasant if she really thought about it.

Which was exactly what she was not supposed to do.

She growled at herself, her bear was woefully quiet at the moment which wasn't that fair, seeing as it was both of their problems. But her bear seemed content to sit this existential crisis out.

Birdie slammed the door shut behind her and when she locked it she tried not to think too much on why she did. She got ready for the auction as carefully as she was able to while keeping an eye on the clock. There was nothing Elodie Salazar liked less than arriving to an event late. She liked it even less when it was her daughter that was doing it. Birdie hopped into her heels, and nearly ate shit going down the stairs in her sprint for the door. She'd rather risk a broken neck than have her mom on her case about the dang auction.

She knew why her mother was going to be pushing her to be on time. She was hopeful Birdie would be a good match to the Stronghearts. Even though they were a pain in the ass, there were some strong bears among them that would make a suitable match and mate. She'd never really thought much on it because she'd hoped her mate would find *her.* She paused at the door and sighed. She wished it had gone differently, there was no two ways about that. If her mate had claimed her back, if there had been even an ounce of discussion between them, things could have been different.

She shut the door, tucked her clutch under her arm and then set off at a jog towards the town square a few blocks away. She had just enough time if she didn't stop. The wind whipped, blowing her hair across her face which wreaked havoc on her carefully done curls, but it couldn't be helped. Not if she wanted to make it on time. She was glad she had picked a close fitting dress that was immune to the force of the Autumn wind which seemed to be picking up strength with every step she took. Thankfully, the lights of Main Street came into view and then Town Square a minute later. It was less windy here, a break created by the stage and awnings stretched between the buildings sheltered everyone in the space from the wind. Birdie figured there was a little magic at work too, from the zips of light she caught moving over the material stretched overhead. It was pretty here, much calmer and more peaceful than the wind she'd run through to make it. Music was playing from the stage and the smells of cooked meat and spiced wine from the stalls filled the air.

She smiled as she inhaled. A group of people waved to her from across the way and she smiled, waving back as she walked towards the stage. Kids were laughing and eating treats. She saw the elders from her clan taking their seats towards the front of the stage while they directed the MC on how to best kick events off. Coffee and hot chocolate was being served by the local coffee shop, Barista Witch, at a pop up stall, and all the shops along the square were brightly lit and filled with shoppers. The liveliness of it made her soul sing.

It was the best time of year.

Birdie was almost backstage when she saw him, though. Just like that morning, she stumbled. *Emmett.* She sighed and looked away from him. How was she going to keep her footing every time the big halfling showed his handsome face?

Earlier she guessed she'd stood a chance, even with him showing up at random. Then, he'd looked disheveled and like he hadn't slept all night. On anyone else it would have looked unappealing but Emmett had managed just fine in Birdie's eyes.

But now?

Now it was a different story.

Emmett was dressed to impress for sure. He wore a pair of tailored, gray slacks made to fit him within an inch of his thighs and in a color that made her think of his eyes. A crisp cream dress shirt contrasted. She even saw a flash of a ring, cufflinks and what she knew was an expensive watch on his wrist. She narrowed her eyes. He was using Fae shit to try and catch her attention. Everyone knew the Fae used shiny things like jewelry and coins to get you to walk off the path and do something stupid, like enter one of their rings or strike a bargain with them.

She should have known that when she raised her eyes to his she'd find him looking at her. Even so, it was unnerving to meet his stare from across the square. She raised a hand and self consciously patted at her hair. It had been curled and styled to look elegant but casual, she didn't know how it had fared in her run but she figured it had to be somewhat windswept. That was entirely romantic and chic enough for a date auction, right?

Emmett's eyes left hers, but not to look away. No, the man was taking a closer look at her. His eyes moved slowly down her body, taking in what she was wearing... or not. She swallowed hard from the way he was looking at her, his gaze taking her in like she was something to be savored. She had a feeling he was looking at more than her clothes. Heat bloomed in her chest and she blushed.

"Shit," she whispered. This wasn't good.

"There you are! Oh good, you wore the green dress. You look so good in that color." Her mother's voice rang out and a second later her mother swept her up in a hug. "You look flushed. Are you alright? Where's your coat?"

"I forgot it?"

"Oh, Birdie."

"Sorry, Mama."

Her mother hugged her and ushered her ahead of her. "I know you don't need it, but I worry. Please wear one from now on?" Her mother was right. Shifters ran hot. It's not like they needed the jackets they wore or the beanies really, but they did it to make the humans in town feel a little more comfortable. There was nothing more unnerving than having -20 degrees weather and your neighbors were just fine in shorts and a tee.

"I'm so glad you're on time. I've got my eye on a very eligible bachelor," her mother said, moving close to whisper to her. Birdie turned her head to look at her mother. Elodie Salazar was a stunning woman. Dark eyes and hair, high cheekbones, the classic kind of beauty that had made her father stop in his tracks. It hadn't been her beauty that had brought them together, though. It'd been the spark, the telltale mate bond spark, that had sealed the deal for them. Which, according to her father, was a lucky thing. Because he had walked into a door trying to get a second look at her the first time he'd seen her.

"Fate knew what it was doing that time," he'd confessed

begrudgingly. It was rare to see her father keen to the way of mates, but it was hard not to give credit where it was due when he'd had such a happy union with Elodie. Birdie had wished for nothing more than what her parents had. She frowned and looked down at her feet. How had things gotten so messed up for her?

Her mother gave her arm a tap. "Dear are you listening?"

"Which one is he?" Birdie replied quickly. She smiled brightly to cover her tracks and thankfully her mother bought it.

"That one over there. The dark haired one. Do you see?" she said with a jerk of her chin. "His name is Rafe."

Birdie followed her mother's gesture and immediately saw the shifter she was talking about. Rafe was tall and muscular, thick in the way male bear shifters generally were. He had dark hair neatly parted and combed. He turned their way and she didn't miss the bright smile he sent her way.

"He's cute, right?" Her mother whispered with a wink.

Birdie smiled in spite of herself and gave the Strongheart shifter a tentative smile back.

"He is. What's his deal?" she asked.

"There's no deal. He's of Beta stock, which we know is solid and something to be admired from your father. He's the oldest of his five brothers and is next in line to run the family mining business, so there's no need for you to work at Eric's bar."

She frowned. "I like working at Eric's. You know that. I'm not giving up working at Waites just because you want me to bag a rich bear."

"Stop making me sound like a gold digger. It's called security. You'll be thanking me later."

Birdie harrumphed but didn't say anything else. At least the shifter was cute. He was dressed well enough and there was something to be said about a bear shifter. She understood bear shifters. It would be easy to move between their worlds without the added complication of halflings and Fae magic.

"Is he in the auction?" Birdie asked.

"No, he's not, but I told him my lovely daughter would be when I introduced myself earlier."

She sighed and gave her mother a raised eyebrow. "You definitely already told him to ask me out, didn't you?"

"I didn't, but your father? Yes."

Birdie covered her face with her hands. "Luna save me."

"Security, Birdie. *Security.* A good match will set you up to be close to us and there's a lot worse you could do than a Strongheart."

"I know, mama." She turned to look at the curtain ahead of them. They were backstage now and only those being auctioned off were here. She could hear the MC kicking off the Fall Festival and when there was a small fanfare of music she nodded at her mother.

"I think that's my cue to line up with everyone else," she said, nodding to the left of them as the participants of the auction were lining up. Every clan and pack was represented along with a smattering of humans, which she thought was brave of them. It wasn't that they didn't know shifters, witches and Fae lived among them, but the auction was an event where the more magically inclined members of Oak Fast made themselves known. The humans in the mix were made of sterner stuff than most.

Her mother kissed her cheek and hugged her. "Excellent. Give me your purse and go knock them dead. You look so beautiful. I love what you did with your hair."

Birdie gave her a little wave before she took her place in line and then she waited. They were being sent out in groups of five. It wouldn't be long before it was her turn to take the stage. She could hear the MC doing their best to keep up with bids and she wondered who would bid on her. Definitely the bear shifter her mother wanted her to go on a date with. What was his name again? Reagan? Randall?

No, it was something sexier than that. It had to be. She was sure of it.

She shuffled forward in line, turning over the thought. Why had she handed over her clutch? Her phone was in there. What if he won her bid and she didn't even know his name? She wished she could text her mother and ask exactly who she was supposed to be flirting it up with.

Remi? *Rhys?*

She scowled and rubbed her temples. No, it wasn't either of those. She was so screwed if he won her bid. Maybe she could fake it and greet him with a 'hey you!' and get away with it for a while until he introduced himself. It's not like they'd ever spoken so she *did* have an excuse as to why she wouldn't know his name...even though her mother had probably already convinced him she was the perfect choice for a partner. And it's not like she would be lying to him. Birdie would be a perfect partner. She'd wanted nothing more than a mate, even if it was the chosen type, the kind picked by the person and not the bear.

A chosen mate could be just as good. It was a meeting of the minds. Something practical that could and would build into more with time and nurturing. She'd found her mate and look where that had gotten her?

Rejected and sitting in a Fae witch's cabin at near midnight, that's where.

Fat lot finding her fated mate had done for her when it came down to it. Birdie crossed her arms and tried not to let her mind wander too far down that road. She'd done it and she was lucky Jazzy had agreed to it seeing as she'd been right about Emmett being pissed off.

Birdie's mind went to him. He'd looked like he was on a mission, from the way he was dressed to the way his eyes had moved over her like she was his to look at for as long as he pleased. Her skin tingled and warmed, which just made her frown. She wasn't supposed to notice him and all his shiny little trinkets, or the way he looked at her.

She didn't really care that his hair was hanging loose and falling just so in a way that made her want to drag her fingers through it and mess it up. She had no business touching him. He was no one to her.

"Hey, we're up," There was a nudge at her side and she turned to see Alice beside her. She was a fox from the Silver Clan. Birdie brightened when she saw her friend.

"Where have you been?"

"At the coffee shop. Why didn't you come in for your latte this morning?"

Birdie frowned as they approached the stage. "I got held up."

"With what?" Alice asked.

"Uh...you know, stuff."

"You never miss whipped cream Fridays," Alice pointed out.

"I knowwww, but sometimes life just goes *ka-boom* and you gotta sacrifice what you love the most," Birdie muttered. They stepped out onto the stage and the announcer introduced them with a flourish.

"And let's have a round of applause for our lovely

and handsome eligible bachelors and bachelorettes!" The crowd clapped and cheered, a few wolf whistles sounded and Birdie was about to let loose a whistle of her own when the MC pointed a finger at her.

"And I call Birdie Salazar to come up as our first bachelorette!"

"Crap, why me?" she whispered to Alice, but her friend gave her a little shove.

"Get out there and make some money. I saw that bear looking you over. You'd make a cute couple. I'm just saying," Alice said with a wink.

She blushed hot. Turned out it wasn't just her mother who had a keen eye when it came to making matches. Birdie plastered a smile on her face and walked forward. The bright lights were on her, which made it a little difficult to see much beyond the stage. She swallowed hard and pushed through her nerves, which were new. She had never had a problem any other time she was meant to take the stage for the date auction. She'd been doing this since her senior year of high school, which was about six years ago, and not once had she had the weird butterflies in her belly feeling that made her want to bolt.

"Don't be shy," the announcer encouraged her. They waved her forward. "Come here, dear. Stand here and let these fine folks appreciate you."

Birdie took her place next to them and it was then that she knew exactly why she'd had the feeling that she wanted to bolt from the stage.

Emmett.

She gritted her teeth. Why was it always coming back to that damn fairy?

He was sitting front row, just within her field of vision from the stage. He was in the seat closest to the aisle, but it lined him up perfectly with her. He tilted his head to the side and looked her over with the same slowness he'd done before. It was calculating. Assessing. It told her he was making notes.

But for what?

She raised her chin in defiance. She could tell he had an opinion on her being in the date auction. That much was clear from the way he crossed his arms over his chest and narrowed his eyes. Again, he looked ticked.

What right did he have to be pissed off? *She* was the one who'd had to visit a Fae witch in the middle of the damn night to get a crumb of peace as his mate. No, not his mate. They weren't mates anymore. Birdie gave herself a mental slap. She couldn't think of him like that. That kind of thinking didn't lead anywhere good for her.

"And where shall we start the bidding for an evening with this shy beauty?" The announcer asked and Birdie almost rolled her eyes at them. It's not like she was hiding behind him. She was just trying to find her footing with Emmett glaring a hole in her forehead. The announcer cleared their throat and gave her a sidelong look when it was evident she was locked into a glaring war with Emmett.

"Uhh.., shall we start the bidding at twenty five dollars?" The starting bid was low. Definitely lower than she'd ever started out at before, which meant she had ground to make up. Which was going to be tough with the situation she was in. She'd never dreamed that Emmett would come, or look the way he did. Then there was the whole glaring thing that had her on edge. Birdie blew out a sigh and shook out her limbs. She had to smile and look sassy.

Emmett leaned forward, elbows to his knees. For one wild moment she wanted to scream at him that if he wanted to stare at her so much he could at least take the time to bid. Instead, he was content to watch her squirm without so much as raising his hand to bid five dollars to put herself out of her misery. She jerked back at that thought and looked away from Emmett. Why the hell was she wanting him to bid on her? She would rather stand up here and owe money than have him pay a single cent on her behalf. That's what she should be thinking, right?

She dropped her eyes to her feet and twisted her hands in her skirts. Shit. She didn't exactly know anymore. Usually when she was here for the auction she went on autopilot and fed off the energy from the crowd and bidders. There was also the fact that she usually had a crush gunning to win her date. Now, she was all turned upside down on account of Emmett being here.

"Twenty five here!" she heard a shout and it was

good, but crap. How was she going to get this thing going? Normally, she was confident and had the crowd eating out of her hand while she egged on the date she really wanted. She didn't have that this year to pull her through.

Instead, she had a pissy not-mate and a possible match her mother was pushing, which did give her something to work with, now that she thought on it.

"I hear twenty five, how about thirty?" The announcer asked. Birdie didn't have time to start enacting her plan to entice the Strongheart shifter to bid because it seemed he had a mind of his own.

"A hundred dollars!" The Bear shifter her mother had picked for her appeared like magic in the aisle. Birdie felt a wave of relief wash over her. Thank Luna. She had thought she was going to have to stand up here frozen under the weight of Emmett's unflinching stare while the bids failed to roll in.

A smile spread over Birdie's face and she raised a hand in greeting to the bear that had just rescued her. He was her hero and he certainly looked every bit the knight-in-shining armor with the way he was standing in the middle of the aisle and grinning at her.

"A hundred dollars to Rafe of the Strongheart Clan! Well done, sir. Rescuing a shrinking beauty from a night of playing the bargain basement wallflower!" The MC's loud declaration made Birdie grit her teeth.

She took a side step towards them and kept a forced smile on her face. "Chill out," she whispered out of the corner of her mouth. Why were they making her sound like she was a spinster? She was twenty-four, not one hundred and four. Even if she had been, he could tone it down a bit, couldn't he? At least the idiot had given her the shifter in question's name. It was Rafe.

Raferaferaferafe. She mentally chanted it to herself, committing it to memory as she stood sweating on the stage.

The announcer gleefully ignored her and addressed the crowd with a flourish of their arm. "Now, do I have any takers to challenge the shifter's bid? Or is it going to be a match made in the stars for these two?"

A second went past and then another voice rang out. "A hundred and fifty."

Birdie's eyes went wide as dinner plates. She knew that voice. It was-

"And the town's librarian has entered the fray! An interesting turn of events to be sure!" The MC was downright gleeful but Birdie wanted to throw her heel at the idiot Fae. What was he doing?!

She looked at him to see that he hadn't risen from his seat. Just raised a finger as he stayed in his relaxed position of elbows to knees as he watched her. He was smirking, eyes on her and her alone. Like Rafe, or the announcer clucking away beside her, didn't exist. They could be alone in a room for the way he was looking at her, not in the square with nearly everyone in town around them.

"Two hundred," Rafe exclaimed and Birdie thought the announcer would swoon.

"Did you hear that? Two hundred! And what say you, Emmett Essex? Do you challenge the shifter?"

Essex. Interesting. For all her knowledge of what he had once been to her, Birdie hadn't a clue what his last name was. Essex was...well, she didn't hate it. It was a good name. Emmett Essex. She winced and gave herself another mental slap. She was going to have to pay Jazzy a visit and demand a refund with the real estate her grandson was taking up in Birdie's mind.

Emmett inclined his head to the announcer. "Three hundred."

A murmur went through the crowd. The hushed whispering and even a gasp had Birdie rolling her eyes. There had been plenty of legendary date auction action before. She'd even been at the center of it her second year in and reached six hundred dollars when the mayor's son had taken an interest in her. Why were they acting like this was a big deal?

"Five hundred," Rafe said without missing a beat and even Birdie's eyes went wide. Okay, so maybe this one was a little sassy.

The announcer leaned forward like they had a secret to tell the audience and Birdie almost swallowed her tongue when she saw the crowd come forward as well to hear what he had to say.

"Did you hear that fair Oak Fast? The hopeful from Strongheart Clan went right to five hundred. What's got him so captivated with our beautiful Birdie? Is it a possible alliance between the clans? They would make a strong couple among the shifter community."

Luna. Did everyone know her mother's intentions with Rafe?

"A thousand!"

Birdie's eyes snapped to Emmett to see he wasn't nonchalant anymore. He was standing and looking at Rafe. His shoulders were squared and she didn't miss the way he lifted his chin in challenge.

She held her breath. Holy hell, he was challenging Rafe right here in front of everyone. She heard the growl from Rafe when he said his next bid.

"Twelve hundred."

The MC gasped into the mic but Birdie wasn't annoyed with them. She got it. *What the heck was going on?* Rafe couldn't want to take her out that badly, could he?

Emmett walked forward until he was only a foot or so away from Rafe. The entire town watched like it was a Shakespearean drama playing out in front of them. The two locked eyes, shifter and Fae and Birdie held her breath along with everyone else in Oak Fast. Emmet was the one to break the stare, but only to look at her.

He pointed at her. "Two thousand dollars for my mate."

Gasps rang out through the crowd. There were voices and exclamations and the announcer howled with laughter. They looked at her and gave her a finger wag like she was a naughty child.

"You kept a big secret from us, my shy beauty! A mate in the bidding war? Of course he's driven to new heights of spending! Two thousand for a date with Birdie! Any takers to challenge her mate? Going once!"

Birdie felt dizzy. Like the ground was swaying beneath her feet. She looked to Rafe to see he was backing away with a frown on his handsome face. She wanted to tell him she was sorry. That she had thought he was cute. That her mother hadn't really been in the wrong with this sort of thing, and that she had absolutely zero control over the Fae he'd been in a bidding war with.

"Going twice!"

Rafe held up his hands signaling that he was done with the whole thing. Birdie pressed a hand to her mouth because she felt sick. Whether it was from excitement or the fact that she was completely freaking out she didn't know yet.

"Going three times! She's gone!" The announcers turned to her and gave her a wink. "Well done, you lucky bear! I didn't know you had a mate. Your mother has some explaining to do at our next night out."

Birdie nodded and when the announcer ushered her to the side, she went. She didn't know what else to do but go in the direction they pointed. Alice was staring at her with wide eyes and she gave her friend a weak smile as their paths crossed.

"When did you get a mate?"

"I don't have one," Birdie whispered to her friend as Alice moved to take her spot on the stage. The fox shifter raised an eyebrow and nodded off to the side. "You might want to tell him that," she whispered.

Birdie looked where Alice indicated. Emmett was off to the side of the stage, hands on his hips and, as always, glowering at her from where he stood. She sighed and repressed the urge to flip him off. He needed to knock off the whole brooding and glaring schtick he had going on with her. He'd gotten them into this whole mess to begin with. She walked towards him with her head high. She was determined not to let the halfling know exactly how much he affected her, even without the mate bond.

She paused at the side of the stage. There was a set of stairs there with four steps in total leading down to where Emmett stood. It wasn't a huge amount of stairs, or a very high staircase, but at her hesitation Emmett came forward as quick as you please and held a hand up to her. Birdie stared at it for a beat and then tucked her hands close to her sides as she descended the stairs on her own. She'd only made it down two though before Emmett's hands closed on her waist and he lifted her right off the stairs.

"What are you doing?!" she yelped as she tried to get away from him, but Emmett was stronger than he looked. Certainly stronger than any human she had met because his grip held fast. "Let me go!"

"No."

She pushed against his hands but Emmett didn't seem the least bit inclined to let her go. "I mean it," she whisper-screamed at him.

"And I meant what I said. No." He loomed over her, his hands still on her waist as he shook his head. "Did you wear this for him?"

Her mouth dropped open. "What?"

"That damn bear."

"No, I wore it for the auction. What are you talking about?"

"Why was he bidding on you like you were his?"

Birdie leaned away from him and, thankfully, Emmett let her take a step back. "My mother thinks we're a suitable match." She didn't know why she was answering him.

"And what do you think?" he asked her. She turned from him and started towards the crowd. She didn't know where else to go, but this was usually where she was sent off with her date for the night after they paid the ladies from the bridge club that manned the donations table.

"I think he's a fine match," she told him quickly. She looked for Rafe. Saw him standing at the back of the audience with a few of the other Strongheart shifters. They seemed to be in deep conversation over the whole thing and she frowned when she saw a couple of them clap him on the back in sympathy. One leaned close and whispered to him and Rafe looked her way. She could see the question in his eyes. Could practically read it from where she stood.

Mate?

She bit her lip and moved to take a step towards him but Emmett was there blocking her. He faced Rafe and when she saw a flash of blue at his hands, that telltale crackle of arcane energy charging the air around him, she grabbed his arm.

"Stop it!"

He turned to her. His gray eyes were alight now with the same kind of blue light that moved around his hands. "He's looking at you."

"A lot of people are looking at me. It's called being in public."

"You are mine."

"Yeah, for the night and that's *it*." She glared at him. "Pay the ladies and let's get this over with." Birdie stomped over to where the ladies at the donation table sat. They were watching them with interest, their silver heads bent together as they whispered. No doubt about what they'd just seen on stage in addition to what they'd just seen happen between Birdie and her supposed mate.

Luna. She thought she'd rid herself of him but now the entire town thought she had a mate. She saw her mother waving at her, trying to flag her down, but she gave her a jerk of her chin. She'd have to explain later. There was no way she was introducing Emmett to her mother. She'd be in over her head if she did that, and she was already *so* over her head. She couldn't afford it.

But like Fate and Fae magic, Birdie really didn't have a choice in the matter and her mother headed straight for them.

CHAPTER SEVEN

"Who is this handsome fellow? A mate?" her mother asked. She was looking between them with the kind of shrewd and calculating look that Birdie was intimately familiar with when it came to matters of her life that her mother did not approve of.

It was no surprise that Emmett thwarting her plans to have Rafe win the auction was one such thing.

Birdie bit her lip and shook her head. "No."

At the same time Emmett answered her mother with a nod. "Yes, that's right. I'm Birdie's mate." He extended a hand to her mother. "I'm pleased to meet you."

"I'm her mother."

"I expected nothing else from your beauty. The pair of you bear a striking resemblance," Emmett said with a charming smile. Birdie's mouth dropped open when her mother blushed and giggled as the halfling pressed a kiss to the back of her hand.

"I'm Elodie Salazar, the Seer for Ironheart Clan."

"He's not my mate, mama," she hissed at her mother, but it didn't do much to damper her mother's fluttering eyelashes, so she tried again. "He's Fae."

That got her mother's attention. "What?" she whispered, eyes wide. She stared at Emmett with new curiosity and Birdie was glad she had the good sense to take her hand away from Emmett who, for his part, didn't seem the least bit bothered.

"A Fae?"

"I'm a halfling, so I wouldn't be too worried," he said with a shrug.

"Still a Fae," Birdie pointed out. "And still not my mate."

"We'll see about that," he told her. "I am her mate. She's just nervous."

Her mother cleared her throat and nodded at him. "When did this happen?" she asked, eyes cutting to Birdie. "Why didn't you tell me this?"

"There wasn't time, mama. I've been busy."

"There's always time for a call when this happens," her mother said with a splayed hand at both of them. "You let me start found mate talks with the Stronghearts. They won't be happy about this," she said, looking over her shoulder at the huddle still surrounding Rafe. "We'll have to smooth it over."

"He doesn't talk to her. I'll deal with it," Emmett

said. His hand came to the small of her back and Birdie took a step away, though it did little for her because he followed her closely. Emmett stayed in her space as he spoke to her mother. "Whatever you promised him, I'll see to it."

Her mother nodded at him, and when she considered him she didn't look so aghast. She looked pleased.

"Negotiations were still in the early stages...I'm sure something could be settled on."

"Consider it done."

"No, do not consider it done. Maybe I *want* to talk to Rafe."

Both her mother and Emmett stared at her.

"You have a mate," they said in unison.

Birdie threw up her hands. "For the last time, I do *not* have a mate."

Emmett growled low. "That's enough of that."

"Birdie, I don't think that's any way to talk to such a generous donator, especially from someone willing to smooth things over with the Stronghearts, now do you?"

Birdie looked at her mother. She could hear the tone in her mother's voice that told her she needed to shape up. She swallowed hard and saw her mother was giving her a 'come on' look. It was true there was going to need to be damage control done with the Stronghearts after the little public display of her so-called mate claiming her in front of everyone, which meant Birdie was pretty much out of luck with her options.

"I think it's time you two went on your date, don't

you? Finish things up with the ladies at the donation booth?"

Two thousand in five minutes was as much money as anyone had ever made in a fraction of the time. Birdie knew her mother wanted to hold on to that as she let everyone know that *of course* she'd known her daughter had a mate.

What mother wouldn't know that?

Okay, so maybe Birdie could have told her mother a little quicker about Emmett and what had happened, but it had seemed too raw to bring up to her family. She'd thought that once she'd gotten it taken care of with Jazzy that she could relax. Just put it out of her mind and live her life for a bit until she was ready, but things really hadn't gone her way lately so she shouldn't be surprised.

"It really was so good of you to bid on her the way you did. We are so grateful! Won't you see your Fae mate to the donations table to pay then, Birdie?" her mother asked and inclined her head to the table with a tight smile.

"Sure," she said quickly. She could tell her mother was worried Emmett might back out. It wasn't out of the realm of possibility when it came to the Fae. They were pernicious. Tricky. Definitely known to find a way to twist every situation to their advantage when the opportunity arose.

But Emmett wasn't exactly ready to go on his way. "Of course, we wouldn't want you to lose face now would we, on account of a flakey Fae. Reputation among the clans comes first, even at the price of your daughter's future, hmm?"

The truth in his words hit close to home. Her mother meant well, Birdie knew that, but there had been talk of her lack of ambition among her parents. They pushed her, as their only child, to achieve. Wished nothing more than for her to be more than she was in the clan and it had always frustrated her. She liked her life the way it was with her working at the bar. She enjoyed her days with plenty of opportunity to go as slow as she liked, because there were always the fast nights full of laughter and friends to look forward to. But that wasn't enough for the Beta and the Seer.

They wanted more for her. *Wanted more from her.*

Birdie wrapped her arms around herself. She wished they could just be happy with what she'd chosen. It was an honest life, even if it was modest. She loved it for those reasons.

Elodie drew herself up to her full height and leveled an impressive stare at Emmett. "I have no idea what you're talking about," she said, but the tense set of her face told the story. Her mother knew exactly what Emmett was getting at.

Birdie cleared her throat. It was time to step in, she decided. The last thing she needed was her mother trying to go toe-to-toe with a Fae. Even a halfling would be a challenge, even for the clan's Seer.

"Mama," she began, but Emmett cut her off before she could get too far.

"Oh, I think you do, and I think you had best reevaluate your priorities, Elodie Seer of the Ironheart Clan. Your daughter's worth cannot be measured by your pitiful clan titles."

Elodie sucked in a sharp breath at the words. Birdie went still because Emmett's eyes were no longer that gray she had come to know, but were black. Black as night. They glittered in the warm glow of the square's lights. Overhead the magic fed twinkle lights flickered, the pattern of shadow and light made it all seem darker. But when she saw the lights over Emmett go out entirely she realized the truth of it.

It was Emmett.

He was the reason for the flickering lights. The shadows crept closer and she was frozen in place, just like her mother. The shadows seemed to draw nearer, wrapping themself to Emmett like a fine suit as he continued to speak.

"Birdie is worth *a thousand times* what I paid to shut that bear up. You don't have to worry about me going back on the deal. A Fae's word is bond. Even if it wasn't, I would never back out of my prize." A look of disdain came over Emmett's face. Even in the shadows Birdie could read it plain as day. The planes of Emmett's face took on a sharper edge, the kind that would have tipped Birdie off that he wasn't entirely human if she didn't already know what she did. "Her value is no reflection of your misjudgment or that idiot on the stage who sold her too cheaply."

Both women's mouths dropped open. Her mother looked like she might say something but Emmett gave her no time for it. Instead he turned to her and gave her his arm.

"Shall we?" he asked. For her part, Birdie was too stunned to protest. So when he slipped his hand over hers and put it in the crook of his arm, she let him. She looked down at his arm as they walked and saw shadows slide over his forearm, up her hands and over her fingers. She shivered but didn't let go of him.

"Hello, dearies! Quite a show you put on there!" One of the bespectacled ladies called out to them. Birdie looked away from the shadows and up to see the women watching them with interest. They were in front of the table, her mother forgotten. The shadows still swirled around Emmett but the ladies watching them with keen interest didn't seem the least bit concerned as they held out their hand for Emmett's payment.

"Two thousand for the pretty little bear."

Emmett was watching her closely. Birdie knew it, but she kept her gaze down on where she was still holding on to his arm. What the hell had she gotten herself into? She had zero experience with the Fae. Sure, she knew stories, but Emmett...the power he was putting off was scary. He silenced even her mother. His grandmother had ripped her mate bond out, though she was starting to wonder about that. There was a tug, the slightest, flimsiest thread of a feeling she could feel there that hadn't been before.

Something was up.

"Are you alright?" he asked her and handed the woman the amount of cash necessary in a stack of crisp one hundred dollar bills.

"Well, isn't that nice," Lou, one of the women who helped her mother at the food bank on Sundays said with a wink. "Bagged yourself a real winner here, Birdie."

"I agree," the other woman said with a titter of laughter. "And he's so handsome too! You ought to thank fate for your good fortune. A mate and a rich one, too!"

Birdie gave them a stiff nod and shuffled off. She didn't know where to go because as much as she didn't like it, she was stuck with Emmett for the night. He'd already thrown the veritable gauntlet down with her mother and she knew better than to go back on a deal with the Fae. There were three things she knew to be sure when it came to fae folk.

Never play a game with the Fae.
Never break an oath to the Fae.
Never ever go into the forest alone with the Fae.

Her idiot self was already alone, or very nearly alone with Emmett. She couldn't break the oath, which she figured was up to interpretation, he and Jazzy had already laid the law down for that one. A business deal was an oath. He'd won the bid for her date, and that counted as a business deal of sorts. It had to with the way he'd referred to it only moments before.

"Birdie is worth a thousand times what I paid to shut that bear up and you don't have to worry about me going back on the deal. A Fae's word is bond."

She didn't want to like that as much as she should. Logically, Birdie knew she shouldn't like it at all. Emmett was wearing fucking shadows for crying out loud, but still. It did do wonders for the memory of her rejection.

She peeked up at him through her lashes while he paid. When he noticed her looking at him he smiled at her. Just a quick upturn of his lips before he was back to listening to whatever it was that Lou had just said.

But that flash of a smile was enough for Birdie to know she was in deep shit.

A Fae's word is bond.

No, he'd said that for a reason. She was stuck on this date until the end. Otherwise, she didn't think she was going to get very far in getting out of her situation with Emmett. There would be no oath breaking happening here. Not tonight. Not ever.

Because for all the caution Birdie had received from her clan elders on what *not to do* with the Fae, she had zero idea what price she would have to pay if she dared break one of the three rules. Emmett's hand moved to the small of her back and she looked up at him. The

shadows still clung to him, the light around him damp-
ened slightly. Even the green of her dress seemed
darker.

"A date deserves dinner. Don't you think?" he asked
her. His eyes were on her mouth as he spoke and she
nodded.

"Sure."

Whatever the price was, Birdie was sure it wouldn't
be good.

CHAPTER EIGHT

"You work here?" Emmett asked her. They were outside of Wildin' Waites. Inside the party was in full swing. She could hear laughter and raised voices. The clink of silverware and the scrape of chairs floated out on the night wind when the door opened and a couple left arm in arm.

"Yeah, you got a problem with that?" she asked him. She was used to the raised eyebrows from some people. Her parents especially, but when Emmett shook his head she was surprised.

"No, it's a good bar. Owner has a decent whiskey selection."

She blinked in surprise. He was right. Eric did have a killer whiskey collection. She'd sampled some the night she'd gone to see his grandma, but she didn't dare tell him about that.

"And good food. There's the Fall Festival menu right now. It's special."

"Right. The menus you were giving out when we met."

That was an interesting way of saying it. *When they met.*

Not when he rejected her and she day shifted out of desperation. She hadn't given her skin to her bear in years like that. Not since she'd learned to control it as a teen. Coming face to face with your mate and having them run the other way had a tendency to rock a girl's control.

"Yeah, I was," Birdie agreed and, because she didn't want to think about that day much, she went on, "I promised Rosie and Eric that I'd come this way with my date. Make him buy dinner, drum up some business and all that."

"I'll take you anywhere you like. If that's this place then let's go inside. It's cold and I don't want you outside any more than you need to be." He frowned and looked her over. "Where's your coat?" he asked.

"Shifters run hot. I don't need one," she reminded him as they walked to the door.

Emmett moved in front of her to open the door. "I don't care what shifters do and don't need. I care about what you need."

"I'm a shifter."

"You're also my mate."

She made a face. "I am not. I paid four hundred to

get that taken care of," she told him and sailed past him into the bar. Behind her she heard Emmett make a strangled sound.

"That's all?"

"What?" she asked, squinting towards the kitchen and bar area. The place was full, every seat packed and everyone seemed to be having a blast. She spotted Rosie by the register chatting away with a customer. Eric walked past carrying a tray of drinks and nodded at her.

"Table in the corner is open," he told her. "Go over and Rosie will come by in a sec."

"Thanks!" Birdie gave him a bright smile and raised a hand in a wave to Rosie who had noticed her.

"You're telling me she did what she did for *four hundred dollars*?"

Birdie shrugged. "I guess so."

"There are college textbooks that cost more than that."

"She said she liked my manners," she told him as they navigated their way through the crowd. She smiled seeing the table Eric had mentioned. It was out of the way at least, which was good because she wasn't too keen on anyone staring at her with Emmett. She knew once word got out about the auction people were going to stare.

Plus, there was the whole bit where he could control shadows. That was going to attract some stares all right. She hurried towards her chair, but when she went to pull it out Emmett was already there. He pulled her seat out for her and, for the umpteenth time that night, Birdie stumbled. She caught herself on the table though, which was a saving grace.

"Uhh..." She hesitated, not sure what to do when he made no move to go to his seat.

He inclined his head. "Ladies first."

She gave him a stiff nod. Right. Manners.

"Thank you," she said in an effort to use hers. Even if she was trying to get off this date without breaking her word, it didn't mean she couldn't be polite. That had scored her major points with Jazzy, hadn't it? Maybe the Fae had an obligation to respond to manners or something?

She hadn't thought Emmett all that kind or polite when she'd first met him but there could be something to that line of thinking. It had worked on his grandmother so why not him? And in any case, given Birdie's lack of knowledge on the Fae, it seemed as good a bet as any when dealing with Emmett and their "date."

She took her seat and tried to ignore the way his fingers lingered near her arm and the heat she could feel on her skin, the soft drag of his fingertips as he moved away from her that made Birdie's head spin. She bit her bottom lip and looked down at the table rather than at him. If they looked at one another she'd probably give herself away that his touch affected her with the blush she had on her cheeks.

She rubbed the palm against the spot on her arm he'd touched.

"Are you alright?" Emmett asked as he settled into his seat. "You look cold."

Shit. He'd noticed.

Birdie lifted her eyes to his. "I'm fine," she lied. She snatched up the menu that lay in front of her. "Do you know what you might like?"

Emmett chuckled. "Yes, I know exactly what I'll have tonight." His words were innocent but they felt anything but. Dark, lush, and with the particular kind of promise that told you there was only delicious trouble ahead. What the hell could he be ordering that had him sounding like that? Against her better judgment Birdie looked over the menu to see he wasn't looking at a menu like she was. He was studying her. His meaning was clear.

He meant her.

"Uh," Birdie said because words failed her. She didn't know how to respond. This was almost as bad as her constant fumbling and tripping when he was around. *Luna!* She wasn't like this. She was confident in herself. At least, she normally was. She didn't act this way with men. It didn't matter that Emmett was apparently only half human, it was the damn principle of the matter. She needed to get her shit together.

"The tapas trio is really good," she settled on and looked back down at her menu. She could do short and sweet. She was beginning to find that back talking a Fae was just the thing to tempt them. Maybe if she ignored it and pretended nothing was wrong he'd lose interest.

There had been that woman after all, hadn't there? That had to be a way to throw him off.

"How's your girlfriend?" she asked nonchalantly as she perused the menu. She'd have the steak sampler. Rare, of course. Maybe a glass of red wine to go with it. Rosie would know just the thing to pair it with. She looked over to see her friend making her way over to them through the crowded bar. Thank Luna.

She'd order, slip out to the restroom and wait there until the food was served. If she dined and dashed, she'd technically fulfill the auction requirements of a date without actually having to be on a date, which meant no oath broken.

It was genius.

She was a genius.

Birdie smiled broadly and gave herself a mental pat on the back at her new plan, but her smile only lasted a second longer before Emmett spoke.

"I don't have a girlfriend. I think you know that, mate."

Her eyes cut to him. "You don't have a mate. Shame about the girlfriend, you seemed cozy." She almost clapped a hand over her mouth. What the actual hell was she doing? Hadn't she just made a pact with herself not to challenge him? Why couldn't she keep her mouth shut?

Emmett leaned forward, elbows on the table and he smiled at her. "Jealous?"

"You wish."

"Oh, there's a very many great things I wish for. I can show you, if you let me," he said.

Birdie nearly swallowed her tongue at the way he looked her over. Emmett was handsome, but he was also...pulling her in. It felt like she was a magnet, and she was the bit of metal caught up in it all, helpless to resist what was happening between them. All she wanted to do was get closer to him, even though she knew it was a stupid, *stupid idea*.

"Oh, I think I know better than that," she replied.

"I see it'll take a little convincing, won't it?"

"Not just a little. Try a lottle."

"How about a game then? A bet?"

Immediately Birdie's alarm bells went off. Fuck. The game. Here it was. He must know exactly what she shouldn't do with him. Why else would he be bringing this up so randomly?

"I think we both know that's a terrible idea."

He tilted his head to the side. "For whom?"

She rolled her eyes and put her menu down with a solid smack on the table. "Me, of course."

He nodded, stroked his chin and looked as if he were considering her words. She knew better though. All of this felt too neat. He knew she would be at the auction. He'd just so happened to have the exact amount needed to win her date. He was bringing the game up when she'd only thought of how emphatically she should not do that with him.

Damn Fae magic.

This was part of his plan. It had to be. She just wished she knew how to get out of the trap that was so obviously being laid for her.

"Can you read my mind or something?" she asked, because it was a rumor they could. He could lie to her, but she wanted to think she could tell if he did.

He chuckled and gave a slight shake of his head. "No. That's an old wives' tale."

"Then why the game?"

Emmett raised an eyebrow. He was interested. "Oh, so games are on your mind then, sweet mate?" He moved closer, leaning over the table as he spoke to her. "Because there are a few I would love to play with you."

Birdie's skin flushed and her dress felt like it was too tight. She took in a short breath and then another because it felt like she couldn't breathe right. The pulse at the base of her throat danced wildly and she swallowed hard as she tried to think through her next move. Every word seemed important. Like she was moving her pieces across some invisible chessboard Emmett was keeping track of with precision while she stumbled along blindly.

She sucked in a breath and then nodded at him. "Oh, I bet you would love that, wouldn't you? Okay, I'm listening, Emmett. What's the game and what do I win if you lose?"

"I won't lose, beloved."

She gritted her teeth at the endearment that made her heart rate triple. "I said, what do I win?"

"You get to leave this date." He inclined his head to the door. "I know that's what you've been plotting to do since we set foot in here. Isn't that right?"

Lying wasn't going to get her anywhere when it came to Emmett so she nodded. "That's right."

"So we play. You win? You get to leave and keep all that cash I know your mother is crowing about to anyone that'll listen and you know what? I'll still see to that bear." He said the last word like it was dirty and she rolled her eyes.

"I'm a bear, you know that, right?"

He inclined his head to her and gave her a smile. "Ah, yes, but you're *my bear*."

She glared at him. He had no right trying to behave like he hadn't rejected her. And Luna, she hated how much she could feel the delicate thread, the thin and reedy thing she knew went from her to him, was that much stronger now than it had been at the start of the night. Mates were a magic all their own, and Birdie knew that magic was made stronger by the time mates spent with one another. Whatever was happening between her and Emmett, the feelings that were waking up in her, had to be because of their time together.

She had to get off this damn date and she had to do it now. She could go back to avoiding him once she was free of it.

"I'm not your anything," she hissed at him and then tapped the table. "Fine. Name the game and let's get this going, because I was going to hide in the bathroom but this seems a lot faster than trying to run down the clock."

"I'm so glad you're seeing things my way. It's easier if you do."

Birdie rolled her eyes at him. "You're a pain in my ass."

"Oh, don't start talking sweet to me now, beloved."

Birdie sucked her bottom lip between her teeth and shook her head. She stared at Emmett who seemed content to look right back. He didn't seem the least bit phased by the glare on her face, but of course he wasn't. This was all part of his plan for the night. It had to be.

"Hi you two! What can I get you?" Rosie's voice broke the tension between the couple. Birdie jumped slightly because she'd forgotten all about her friend or dinner really. Emmett, on the other hand, was calm as a cucumber. He turned to Rosie like he'd been expecting her and smiled in greeting.

"Good evening, Rosie. I'd like to start by apologizing for the last time you saw me."

Her friend, for the most part, seemed determined to have Birdie's back even if she knew messing with a Fae was bad news.

"You mean when you were with your girlfriend?"

Birdie felt a bloom of affection for Rosie. She absolutely loved the awkward question.

"No girlfriend. I did make sure to clear that up with my mate tonight," he said, inclining his head to Birdie. Rosie's mouth dropped open at his words. "And I've set on amending my poor showing and behavior towards her, but to do so I need your help. You were there, so you know the ground I have to cover. Will you help me?" Emmett didn't look like the type of man who commanded shadows or wore them like finery. He was every bit the contrite charmer now that he was talking to Rosie. Her friend bit her lip and for one wild second Birdie thought she would hold strong, but then Emmett brought out the big guns.

He dropped his head and managed to look up at her friend through his lashes in the way that particularly large and very sorry men resorted to when they were at your mercy.

"Please?" he asked.

Oh no. She was done for.

Rosie rocked back on her heels. "Well..." she began and Birdie groaned internally. She wanted to reach out and shake her friend and beg her to absolutely not help him but Birdie knew that was a losing battle. Rosie was falling for Emmett's plea. Hook, line and sinker.

"Can you do that for me?" he asked Rosie. Her friend's eyes came to her for a beat before they went back to Emmett's and Birdie wanted to scream. She could see the indecision there. The soft-hearted nature of Rosie was bubbling up to the surface and all he'd had to do was say please.

Fuckity fuck.

"Well, I mean...maybe?" Rosie said. She crossed her

arms over her chest and cleared her throat. "I mean, because of the mate thing."

"Of course, I know you understand how delicate mates are. It's a very important thing. Not to be taken on lightly. I admit, I panicked," he said and looked at Birdie. "I was a fool to throw something so precious away. To run from it the way I did. But I will make it up to my mate."

He meant what he was saying. She could hear it in his voice, the earnest look in his eyes pushed away the side of him that had her on the ropes and feeling out of her depth.

"Of course, I'll help you. I know how it can be scary with mates. You're doing the right thing now and that's what matters," Rosie said. She looked at Birdie meaningfully, and inclined her head, "Right?" she asked her. The message was clear. No help was coming her way from Rosie. Birdie looked away and shrugged with a mumbled reply that was neither a yes or a no, so much as it was a sound.

Damn.

"What do you need?" Rosie asked.

Emmett beamed at her. "I knew I could count on you. The only thing I need to set this right is the bar."

Birdie's eyebrows shot up. What the hell did he mean by *the bar?* Rosie tilted her head to the side as she processed his words.

"What do you mean the bar?"

Emmett straightened and looked around the

bustling space. "I mean the bar. The entire place. I'll need it to make this right," he paused and then added, "plus a deck of cards if you have them. If not, I can manage."

"You want me to clear the bar out?" Rosie asked.

He nodded. "I do, but don't worry. I'll more than compensate for what you'll lose in revenue."

"She can't clear the bar out. It's the first night of the festival. The place is packed and-"

"How does twenty thousand for the night sound?" Emmett asked, interrupting Birdie's speech about why Wildin' Waites couldn't just clear everyone out on one of the busiest nights.

Rosie let out a choked laugh. "What do you mean twenty thousand?"

"For the bar. The night, I mean. I'm sorry this is happening on such a busy night but," Emmett gestured at Birdie, "fate waits for no one and I have the difficult task of turning Birdie's heart and body to me. I have cash if that helps."

Birdie's mouth dropped open. There was a lot to process in what Emmett had just said. First, twenty thousand cash? Who just carried that kind of money on them?

But most importantly.

"My *what*?" she sputtered and held up a hand. "I agreed to a date. What the hell are you going on about 'heart and body?' That is definitely not included in this date."

"*Ah, ah, ah*, remember after the game, beloved."

"That I'm going to win."

Emmett went on as if she hadn't spoken. "After you've lost I'll collect what's mine."

Birdie crossed her arms over her chest. "Which is?"

"A kiss."

Rosie sighed and her hand fluttered to her heart. "Aw, that's really sweet. He wants a kiss," she said, looking at Birdie with a smile. Birdie shook her head. She had spent enough time around Emmett to know it wasn't just a kiss.

There was more to it.

Birdie shook her head. "Rosie, I don't-"

"A kiss that I get to place wherever I want on my mate's beautiful body," Emmett said, looking Birdie over.

"Oh, uh, okay, I take it back," Rosie whispered. Eric came up to her side at that moment and slung an arm around her shoulders.

"Take what back?" he asked and dropped a kiss to the top of her head. He froze when he noticed Birdie and Emmett staring at one another. Emmett with a lazy smile on his face while Birdie looked like she might bolt.

"What's going on here, Petal?" he asked, eyes going between the trio. Birdie crossed her fingers he'd do something. He was a sensible shifter. He knew how the Fae were. Even if it was mate adjacent, she was a part of his clan. He had to help her.

"Mate stuff," Rosie whispered to him and then cleared her throat. "Ah, Emmett wants to rent out the bar to take Birdie on a date."

Eric nodded. "Nice, nice. When?"

"Tonight," she replied and Eric laughed.

"Tonight? Sorry, friend. There's no way that I can do that," Eric said with an apologetic smile and Birdie let out a sigh of relief.

"Thank god someone has some sense here. Thanks for nothing," she said, pointing a finger at Rosie who rolled her eyes at her.

"Oh stop. Mate stuff is important."

Birdie threw up her hands. "You were there when I had the bond ripped right out of me, so don't you even start with me."

Eric watched the two women go back and forth and cleared his throat before he nodded at Emmett. "I can't clear out the bar tonight. Not with the crowd we have tonight and-"

"He wants to pay us twenty grand," Rosie told him. "Cash."

Eric clapped his hands. "Right then!" He looked out at the bar floor and cupped his hands around his mouth. "Everyone clear out! Bar's closed!"

Birdie groaned and slumped down in her seat. The bar went silent and the beginnings of grumblings began, but Eric waved them off. "We're doing our part to get these two together," he said, jerking a thumb back at Birdie and Emmett. "You all understand how mates are," he said with a conspiratorial wink.

"He won her auction for two grand!" A voice called out.

"But I thought she was supposed to be matched with the Strongheart Beta."

"Oh that's just her mother's meddling."

Birdie groaned and slunk down in her seat at the voices she could make out. "Someone put me out of my misery, please."

Rosie patted her shoulder. "Sorry, but I think this is good. You two, can, you know...talk it out."

Birdie opened her eyes to glare at her friend. "You're in big trouble later."

"The party will continue down at Annie's Cantina, and the first round is on me, so pack it up! Let's move it!" Eric clapped his hands again and ushered people towards the door. Birdie would never again underestimate the power a free drink had on an Oak Fast resident as she watched the patrons practically skip towards the bar door, their earlier grumblings long forgotten at the promise of a free margarita.

All too soon they were alone and Emmett slipped from his stool. "I can't thank you both enough," he said looking at Rosie and Eric. He slipped a hand into his pocket and out came a roll of crisp one hundred dollar bills that he handed to Eric. "For your generosity. You can count it if you like."

Eric waved a hand at him. "No need. Your people are honest. I trust the Fae."

Birdie made a choking sound because who trusted the Fae? Eric ignored her and then held up a deck of cards. "Rosie said this was part of the deal."

"Ah, perfect. I thought we might have to improvise but this makes things so much neater. I won't forget this kindness," he said, taking the deck of cards in his hands.

Eric inclined his head to the Fae. "Is there anything you need?"

"Everyone is leaving, yes?" Emmett asked.

"I can have the staff leave with us. Birdie has keys to lock up," Eric said and gave him a thumbs up, already on his way to the kitchen. "I'll have them clear out. You two have a nice night," he said. He held out his hand to his mate and shot Birdie a wink. Rosie stared at his hand and then back at Birdie. She looked like she wasn't sure what to do but when Eric caught her hand she went with him with a mouthed *sorry* at Birdie.

Birdie vowed not to forget or forgive the predicament her friends had put her in. She heard the kitchen door swing shut and a minute later the back door did too. They were alone now. Crap. She cleared her throat and looked at Emmett when she heard him start to shuffle the cards.

"What are you doing?" she whispered. Her voice sounded impossibly loud in the now quiet space. The transition from raucous party to silence had happened so quickly, so seamlessly, that Birdie felt off kilter. It seemed like anything was possible when Emmett was around. He had the power to turn her world upside down with a few words or a quick decision. Just like his snap decision to reject her.

"Preparing for our game."

She frowned and watched him shuffle the deck as he headed back to their table. It seemed odd that he would choose to return to the small table when they now had the bar, but she followed him anyhow to take a seat. Emmett cut the deck and began to separate them into piles.

She took a seat when he did. Why she sat, who knew? Before she knew it she was across from and watching his hands move.

"What game is it?"

"Black Jack. Twenty One. Pontoon," he paused and looked at her. "I can't think of any more human names for it, but I think you get what game I'm going for."

"What do you mean 'human names'. Aren't you human? Well, I mean, aren't you mostly human?"

"I'm half. I'm sure my grandmother referred to me as a *halfling* to you."

Birdie nodded. "She did, but..." her voice trailed off and she thought of the scene with her mother. The way the lights had flickered, how the smell of his magic in the air was like metal and amber. Rich and so alarming that she knew better than to relax into it. She shouldn't be this close to him.

Emmett looked up at her. "But what?"

"You don't seem like one."

"And how many Fae do you know to think that, beloved?"

Birdie licked her lips and Emmett's eyes moved to track the movement. Small as it was, Birdie knew he was committing it to memory. A jolt of want shot through her, the force of it shocking her and making her squirm in her seat. The shifter in her wanted her to run, but if she had the chance she didn't think her bear would let her. As nervous as Emmett made them, leaving was not at the top of her bear's list.

As such, even without the fear of breaking an oath, Birdie was stuck. It was a curious thing. She was usually so in tune with her bear. They were one and the same. It was a point of pride for her to be able to connect so easily with her bear. She knew it wasn't the norm but here she was, finally at odds.

Her bear wanted Emmett. Birdie didn't. Long term, that really didn't amount to much seeing as she'd visited Jazzy, but in the short term it did mean she was stuck where she was.

She shifted in her seat and shrugged as she answered him. "Enough."

"How many is enough?"

"What does it matter?"

"It matters to me who my mate has been seeing." He set the cards down on the table in front of them and then moved his hand quickly, fanning them out in an arc across the polished wood. "It matters to me what Fae might have seen you and had the thoughts I've had cross their mind."

Birdie shouldn't ask. She knew she shouldn't, but Luna, she couldn't help herself.

"And what thoughts are those?"

Emmett smiled at her and tapped the table in front of her. "I'd rather show you, beloved. Why don't you pick a card?"

Birdie hesitated. Her eyes went down to the cards that lay on the gleaming table and she considered. She might ask if they could play a different game, but that hadn't been in their agreement, which was on her. She knew better than to agree to play a game with the Fae. She really should have taken more care with her words, so the fact they were playing a game she didn't choose was to be expected. Thankfully, the rules were simple.

Get as close to 21 without going over. She could do that.

Anyone could do that.

If she managed it the date was over and she could slink back to her apartment and regroup from this night. Nothing had gone right, not since the auction. She looked up at Emmett and bit her lip. He looked utterly at ease, so maybe things had only been going wrong for her. Every twist and turn of the evening had seemingly played out in Emmett's favor after all. Maybe it didn't matter what she did during this game. Not really.

She raised her hand and moved close to the cards.

Her fingers hovered over a card to the middle and then one out to the side. "I don't understand why you're here," she told him and then tapped a card. Emmett flipped it over for her.

"Queen. Not a bad way to start," he told her. Emmett looked up at her. "I'm here because you're my mate. I'm here to fix a mistake."

She bit her lip. A face card automatically meant ten points. Shit, she was going to have to watch her next draw. He moved his hand over the card spread and tapped a card. Birdie flipped it for him.

"Ace of spades," she said with a nod. The score was at least in her favor. 10 to 11, she had more room to work with. Maybe she could pull this off. "You didn't think it was a mistake when you did it," she told him.

He shrugged as if it were an honest mistake. "I was caught by surprise, beloved. A mate was not something meant for me. I was overwhelmed at what was happening. My human half took control. I'm terribly sorry."

She frowned at him and moved her hand over to another card. She gave it a tap. "What do you mean your human half? And the Fae have mates all the time, so why not you?"

Emmett flipped her card over for her.

"King," he said as Birdie began to do the mental tally. 20 to 11. She was doing okay. The last round of their cards to draw was coming on fast now, but she didn't want it to end just yet. She could sit here and not draw another card and probably win this thing, but instead of exhilaration, she felt a wave of disappointment.

Why did she feel that? Shouldn't she be excited about that?

She'd been tempted into a game and her win was in sight. All she had to do was be patient and she'd be off this date. Birdie frowned at the thought. Nothing made sense when she was near Emmett. Birdie rubbed her temple and sighed. Why was she upset about winning?

"I'm part of a very old line. One that was punished for a very long time," he told her.

"How were they punished?" she asked before she realized she was speaking.

Emmett hummed, fingers skimming the cards in front of him. For one wild moment Birdie wanted to cover his hand with hers and stop him from picking his next card. She wanted to know the story of Emmett and his people. Or maybe it was more. She wanted more time with him. The urge came over her quick and sudden, and the intensity of it had her pressing her hands close to her thighs to keep from reaching for him.

"My great-great-great-grandfather took a mate that was not his to have. It earned him a curse that was passed down through the line, one by one, until the debt had been paid."

Birdie sucked in a breath. "Who cursed him?"

"Our Queen."

"Your own queen cursed your family for something you didn't do?"

Emmett gave her a slow nod and tapped a card in front of her, but Birdie didn't look to see which one it was. "She has a unique brand of justice, but yes. She cursed us to go without our fated mates, our true mates, until the debt was paid by what my ancestor stole. He has not lived it down even after all these centuries."

Birdie's eyes went wide. "He's still alive?"

"In a way," he said in the all too frustratingly cryptic way that the Fae had when it came to answering questions they didn't care to. "You didn't flip my card," he told her.

"Oh, right, right," Birdie murmured and then looked down at the cards sheepishly. "Which one was it?" she asked.

"This one here," Emmett said as he placed his hand on hers. A spark went between them, the silvery flash of it there and gone again so quickly Birdie might have missed it. She knew Emmett hadn't missed it, not from the way his hand tightened on hers, but he didn't comment on it. Instead he moved her fingers to his card.

"I never thought I'd have a mate. Then one day, it was you. I panicked. I thought it was a cruel joke."

She flipped the card. "Six of diamonds," she said softly. The score was 20-18. She could stop. Just let it ride and win. If she did, Emmett would be forced to draw a card for a chance to win and only a three could win the game. Only one card would win it for Emmett.

While all Birdie had to do was sit tight and not do anything stupid.

Emmett hadn't moved his hand from hers, his touch was warm against the back of her hand and fingers.

"Why would it be a joke?"

"Like I said, our queen has a unique sense of justice. I thought that if-" Emmett began and then broke off with a sigh, "I don't know what I thought at that moment, or what would happen if I let you in. If I claimed you as my mate. I thought if I did then you would be gone from me. Taken."

"If you thought that, then why have you been trying to claim me now?"

He moved his hand away from hers. "Because when my grandmother took the bond out of you, I felt it in my soul. It was like I was cracked wide open and there was nothing left of me. Nothing without you. I knew then the bond was real. It wasn't a joke or trick. Not a debt to pay for my grandfather's decisions, but real. You were real, Birdie. And it was me that lost you." Emmett's shoulders slumped and it made her heart ache.

She knew she was supposed to watch herself with him, but here she was playing a game...she swallowed hard. You'd think managing not to play a game with a Fae would be easily done. It's not like there were many circumstances that demanded a game with a Fae, and yet, here Birdie was, sitting where she was, in a game of Black Jack. She dropped her eyes to the cards in front of her. She chanced a look at Emmett and saw that he was looking at her, not the cards.

"Are you going to play the next hand?" he asked.

Her chest went tight. She knew she didn't have to play the hand. If she did, then there'd be nothing to keep the night from ending. If she didn't play, the night was over. That had been the whole point of it, right? A game with Emmett in exchange for her freedom. She swallowed hard and reached out, fingers hovering over the cards. She wasn't thinking, she was reacting. Moving on instinct as her fingertips dragged over the backs of the cards.

It was then she realized she hadn't thought she'd win. Or maybe it was that she hadn't *wanted* to win. She didn't know. It was all mixed up when it came to her not-mate. If she played this round then the odds were against her. She was betting on losing with only an ace winning the game for her. She hesitated. If she played, she was willingly stepping into the trap Emmett had set out for her.

"You don't have to play this hand. You know that, right?"

It would be a stupid thing to play the hand. She knew it. By Emmett's question, he obviously knew it as well.

Birdie's eyes went up to Emmett. He was watching her closely. The slightly broken softness that had been in him just a moment before was gone. The dark-eyed

Fae that commanded shadows and paid a stupid amount of cash to spend time with her was back.

She inclined her head towards him. "I know."

"I thought you wanted to win," he said.

She never claimed to be smart. Her family could attest to as much, so Birdie did what she did best. She did something stupid.

Birdie dropped her fingers to the cards and gave one a tap. "Who says I'm not?" she whispered.

CHAPTER NINE

Birdie didn't know who moved first. It could have been her or Emmett, but everything happened in a blur. In a rush. The kind that came on you when everything was heightened, acute and sharp like the first winter snow on your skin. The sharp bite of pine needles beneath her bare feet when she ran under the moonlight. That same sort of fluidity and technicolor was fully present in her bear.

That was here now.

Emmett wrapped his arms around her as he lifted her up out of her seat and carried her forward. Unlike not knowing who moved first, Birdie knew damn well who kissed the other first. It was her. She kissed him, turned her face up to his and pressed her lips against his with a moan.

Emmett's mouth slanted to hers, his tongue slid across the seam of her lips and she opened to him. The kiss deepened and she moaned again as Emmett swallowed the sound down eagerly. He nipped her bottom lip and she laughed. Kissing Emmett wasn't like when she was trying to watch herself around him. Not like when she felt acutely aware of the missteps she was in danger of making. Kissing him was...effortless. It felt exhilarating, the slide of his tongue against hers, the press of his lips, the way his hands were firm on her hips as he held her up. They fit together perfectly. There were no bumped chins or noses, no instance when she might clack her teeth to his, even when their touching reached a fever pitch.

There was only the kind of joy that made her aware she'd never had this before. That it had never been quite right with anyone until now. That the kisses and touches Emmett was giving her were far beyond what she'd known.

Birdie's back came up against the counter and then a second later Emmett was lifting her onto the bar. She hadn't even realized they had crossed the room from their table.

"What are you doing?" she asked when he settled her onto the bar top. It was a surface she touched every day, one that she cleaned and served drinks on during her shifts at the bar, but she'd never thought it as interesting as it was in this moment. Emmett came closer to her and his body pushed her thighs apart as he came to settle between them.

"What are you doing?" she whispered again. Her

voice came out in a rasp and she swallowed hard as she stared down at Emmett. His hands were on her thighs, the dress she'd worn hiked high so that his palms cupped her flesh.

"It's time for my kiss."

"I-I-" her words came out in a stammer. She didn't know what to say, not with Emmett looking at her like he was from between her thighs. He dropped his head, nose brushing across her skin as he inhaled.

"You smell sweet, beloved."

Birdie wiggled her hips closer to the edge of the bar top and pressed her palms flat to the counter. "Emmett, please."

His eyes met hers. "Please what?"

She bit her bottom lip. She knew she should hold back the words. That she shouldn't ask for what she wanted, but it was impossible not to. Birdie was powerless to resist the pull she felt.

"Kiss me."

Emmett's eyes drifted closed and he moaned. The sound vibrated the side of her thigh and she whimpered. She knew she was wet for him. Her panties would show the proof of it if Emmett checked for himself. Not that he would need to. Her arousal was in the air. Thick and rich. Even if he wasn't as attuned to scent as she was, he would have known just how much she wanted him.

Even so, he moved closer to her, inhaled deep with a

moan. "Beloved," he groaned, eyes closed and lips pressed to her thigh.

"Emmett, I...I...please," she whispered. She reached out and slid a hand through his hair until they caught in his hair and she tugged him closer to her. She knew she'd be embarrassed later, but she didn't have it in her right now. The only thing she knew was the desire for her mate that overwhelmed her, that made her lose all sense. It was the only word going through her mind that made sense.

Mate.

Mate. Mate. Mate. Mate. Mate.

She'd felt this once before in the library. Again, when she'd seen him on the street. And here it was again. The feeling she'd run straight from was bearing down on her with such exquisite pressure that even if he didn't have her pinned to the bar top she wouldn't have been able to move a single muscle in the opposite direction of Emmett.

"I know," he murmured. His voice was low and *Luna*, she felt his words rumble against her skin. It drove her mad. It made her wild and she arched her hips to him, offering herself as best she could.

"Touch me." She swallowed hard and looked down at him where he was poised between her thighs. His lips were just above where she wanted. Her dress was rucked up, the skirt of it flared around her waist and spilled over the shiny wood she sat on. The thin material of her panties and the scant space between them was the only thing that separated Emmett from her aching pussy. She was wet, soaking now and when she moved closer to him she felt it spread over her thighs.

She ached. The pain of her need was sharp and piercing through the high she was getting from allowing herself to be this close to him, especially after fighting it as hard as she had. She didn't know if it was the right thing to do, not logically, but instinctually?

This was exactly where she needed him to be. Where they both needed to be. Birdie's fingers in his hair tightened and then she did the thing she promised herself she wouldn't. She begged.

"Emmett, I need you. *Please.*"

"Beloved."

Emmett's grip on her tightened and his fingers dug into her thighs. She gasped from the bite of his touch, but it was also exquisite. There would be bruises later from where he was touching her but she wouldn't mind those reminders of his touch. He turned his head and pressed his nose against her. He moved to settle a hand over her, fingers splayed out possessively as he slid her panties to the side. Emmett pressed a kiss to her exposed flesh, and then another, until he was tasting every inch of her. Birdie moaned when she felt the slide of his tongue through her folds. He took his time in his exploration of her, tongue slowly thrusting in out of her while he mapped the shape of her. She fell back on her elbows to watch him. He was a beautiful sight between her thighs, long hair gleaming under the light as he thrust two fingers into her. His other hand moved up, lightly skimming her over sensitive flesh while Emmett peppered kisses over the path his fingers took. He pressed a kiss to her clit and that was when he looked up at her.

"Oh fuck," Birdie gasped when he sucked her clit into his mouth. He didn't look away from her, and for her part, Birdie was transfixed. His attention on her, the focused and intense way the Fae between her thighs watched her as he worked her body, had her unable to look away from him. She loved the way he watched her. She wanted him to watch her. She wanted to greedily drink up every second of it. Commit it to memory and revisit it later when this was over.

He moaned, the taste of her on his tongue was making him close control. She could tell from the way his eyes were going black. That dark and glittering Fae that had purchased her at the date auction was here again. His face took the sharper edges she'd only just glimpsed and, while it had frightened her before, it had the opposite effect now.

Pleasure coiled in her belly, it spread through her body with the speed and intensity of a winter storm rolling off the mountains. He was greedy for her. Possessive. She was bringing the Fae side of Emmett to the surface and she loved it. Shadows moved closer, they pulsated around them and then loomed close at Emmett's back. They darkened and formed, coming fully into sight as so much more than just shadows and, suddenly, she realized what they were.

Wings.

He had wings. Gorgeously dangerous and black. They curled close around her until the lights overhead were muted and almost nonexistent. Emmett's wings blocked everything out but him. Birdie's world narrowed until it was only Emmett. He was the only thing she could see, the only thing that seemed real, in this world of shadow.

"Emmett, I-I-!"

She didn't know what she was trying to say, or might have said. She was babbling, the only real coherent thing able to come from her his name. Emmett curled his fingers and changed the angle of his fingers inside of her. He sucked her clit harder, just the right amount of roughness, enough to make her see stars and lose all good sense. Her arms shook and gave as she fell back onto the bar and let the wave of ecstasy roll right over. It caught her up like an undercurrent and swept her over the edge and she climaxed with a scream.

"Emmett!"

He wrapped an arm around her thigh and held her close to him, her thigh to the side of his head as he continued to devour her. He pushed her along, forced her to ride wave after wave of pleasure until she was sobbing and gasping. She pushed at his shoulders and moved to get away.

"I can't," she sobbed. "It's too much."

"One more, beloved. Give me one more," he growled against her slick pussy. He moved close, tongue thrusting into her, licking up her cream with a satisfied moan. Birdie almost told him she couldn't, that it wasn't possible for her to, but like so many things that had happened between them, Emmett showed her just how wrong she was.

CHAPTER TEN

When Birdie woke up the next morning she was pissed.

"What the fuck did I do?" she moaned and turned over, shoving her face into her pillows. The memory of last night greeted her the second she'd opened her eyes.

"You idiot." She gave her pillow a punch and lay there. How could she have done what she had?

It wasn't so much that she'd gotten physical with Emmett. Hell, she wasn't even that upset that she'd done it on the bar top she spent her days cleaning and serving drinks at. That wasn't what made her mad and wanting a whole do over on the past twenty-four hours.

It was that she had opened herself right back up to what she'd tried to put the kibosh on. Her mate bond. The proof of it was there, pushing right up against her chest.

Right above her heart. The mate bond she'd had Jazzy see to was alive and kicking, thrumming with energy and power like it had always been there. She pushed herself up from under her pillows with a scowl when she felt a tug.

"Wait a minute," she whispered and pressed a hand to it. The once thin thread and barely there bond, the one she'd felt spring to life on Main Street, was vibrant now. And more than that, she could feel it pulling on her.

That meant Emmett was pulling on it. She frowned and stared down at her chest expecting to see something there, anything, but there was nothing to give proof to the tug she felt. Why was he yanking on it? She concentrated and reached out with a hand. Even though she couldn't see it, she could feel it. She plucked a finger across it and when she had an idea of where it was, wrapped her other hand on it and yanked back as hard as she could.

"Let's see how he likes it," she muttered. She moved off her bed, determined to go through her normal morning routine and not pay anymore mind to the pull in her chest. Not until she could sort through what she was feeling. Things had changed last night. She knew that. And it wasn't just that she'd given over to the attraction and need she'd felt for Emmett. She wasn't mad at herself for that. But now things were more complicated than she'd anticipated.

What was she supposed to do with a mate? He

swore he would win her, prove to her that she was the one for him but...could she trust it?

Beloved.

Her heart gave a lurch when she remembered the way that word sounded coming from him. It was intoxicating to think of. And the focus he'd given her when he'd brought her to orgasm, not once, not twice, but Luna knew how many times, was dizzying. Her face flushed and she had to fan herself thinking about Emmett's need to make her come. By the end of it she'd been worn out and exhausted, deliriously floating on a cloud of pleasure that made her feel drunk. There had been no way she could have walked home afterwards, which was fine by Emmett.

He'd carried her home through the now quiet streets of Oak Fast. Carried her as if she weighed nothing as he held her close. All the while whispering in her ear the entire way home.

"You were beautiful for me, beloved."

"Do you know how sweet you taste?"

"I'm so proud of you, my beautiful mate."

She swallowed hard and shook her head. She had to focus. Birdie had big things to think about. Now wasn't the time to get lost in last night, no matter how fucking dreamy or hot it had been.

Could she trust him?

What if she gave into him and he rejected her again?

"I never thought I'd have a mate and then one day, it was you. I panicked. I thought it was a cruel joke."

His confession made her pause. He'd told her exactly why he'd rejected her and tried to get away from their fated mate status. She understood it. Really, she did. But that didn't change the fact that she wouldn't be able to take it if he did change his mind. What if it was too much for him down the line? What if he was over-whelmed again? She'd pulled through the first round of all of this because the bond hadn't been sealed, their connection had been in its beginnings and she could endure it then, but now?

Birdie already knew that last night had taken them somewhere bordering on irreparable. One wrong deci-sion now would send her moon-touched. She'd lose it. Like the ferals in the woods that bordered their terri-tory without a pack. She ran her hands through her hair and sucked in a deep breath. She couldn't let that happen.

She loved her life here in Oak Fast. She wouldn't lose her clan, or herself, to a broken bond. Another tug came through the bond and she gritted her teeth. Just because it was here between them didn't mean it had to stay. If she paid another trip to Jazzy maybe the old witch could help them come to an agreement that worked for everyone. She dressed quickly and ignored the incessant pull of her bond. It felt like Emmett was trying to call her to him. Why, she didn't know, but she tried to keep her mind from it.

If she acknowledged it, she'd go to him. She couldn't do that. Not until she had a plan in place. She winced at the incessant pull as she descended the stairs and left her apartment. She hesitated on the sidewalk and looked at her door before she sighed, took her keys out and locked it. Birdie tried not to think too much on the particulars of why she locked it, or how it would make a certain halfling happy she had done it. She went to her car, the destination of Jazzy's cabin firm in her mind and was well on her way out of town when the unthinkable happened.

Emmett.

He was there, or at least she thought it was Emmett. If she hadn't had the bond in her chest humming along, flaring to life with such a force that made her gasp, then she might have mistook the figure that appeared beside her car as someone else. Something else, really. Because for it to be a *someone,* it had to be a person.

And people didn't fly. They didn't have impossibly huge black wings that blocked out the morning sunlight.

But Emmett did.

She looked over and there he was, flying right alongside her car with the shadows she knew to be his enveloping him and her car.

"Fuck!" Birdie cried out. The shadows made it impossible for her to see the road. "What the hell are you doing?!" she yelled at him through her open window.

"Pull over!" Emmett roared at her. *"Now."*

"I can't see the road, you asshole!" she hollered back

at him. Though a second later, she knew it didn't matter that she couldn't see because her car was lifted right off the road. If that wasn't enough, she felt the power go right out of it. It didn't matter how hard she pressed the accelerator, her car was dead.

She glared at him through the open window. "Damn it, Emmett!"

"I know where you're going and it's *not* happening, beloved."

Her car came to a stop. The jolt of him moving it to the side of the road made it rock forward, but Birdie didn't stick around to see what he was going to do next. She was so damn mad at him. Why did he get to make the decisions in their whatever the hell this was?

She leaped from the car the second it touched the ground and took off at a sprint, bursting from the swirling envelope of Emmett's shadows so suddenly she nearly lost her footing at the bright sunlight that hit her.

"Shit." Birdie threw out her hands and caught her balance. She kept running, picking up speed as she bolted for the tree line.

"Birdie!" Emmett's shout rang out across the space between them, it bounced off the firs and pines. She couldn't see him but she knew he was right behind her, no doubt one hundred percent in his Fae form. Wings, glittering black eyes and sharp features. She shivered at the smell of the arcane magic he commanded. The metallic scent was there but there was more, the amber and warm musk she associated with Emmett was stronger. She wanted to turn to him, but forced herself to keep moving.

She deserved the chance to make her choice. He'd made his, and now it was her that was confused. Why was she the one meant to bend where he willed her to?

No, she would run on.

She could cut through this glen and make for Jazzy's once she was in the trees. Red River was south of here. If she shifted she could make the distance in no time, faster now that she had Emmett on her ass.

"Birdie!" Emmett's yell ripped through the morning air and everything around her went still. She knew the wildlife was running from them or taking cover. There was power in his voice. He was a predator. She knew that as surely as the animals in the forest did. She wasn't used to this. The feeling of being prey. As a bear, there were few things that threatened her in the forests surrounding Oak Fast. Precious little in her clan's territory that dared to challenge her.

But for all those few things, Emmett was one of them. She burst through the tree line and shifted. Her clothing ripped and shredded, the remnants of it fell to the ground as she sprinted forward. It was then she realized she'd broken another one of the rules.

Never ever go into the forest with the Fae.

Of all the things she hadn't intended to do, this was the biggest one of them all. She was a shifter and the forests of her territory were her rightful place, but she was far from Iron Tooth lands. She was in the woods no clan or pack claimed. These woods were older, darker, a place she'd been warned away from because of the Fae's claim on them. It made sense, given where Jazzy's cabin was, but she hadn't thought too terribly hard about that before she'd run from Emmett.

She was firmly in his world now.

Shit.

Birdie leaped over a log and crashed through a stream. Branches broke as she plunged ahead. She didn't bother to be quiet or hide her path forward. There was no need to. Emmett would have been able to track her no matter how much care she took, so she chose speed. If she was able to get close enough to Jazzy's cabin she hoped the old witch would intervene. She had once before, so why not now?

She ran for another few minutes before she realized the woods were eerily quiet. She didn't hear Emmett shouting her name, or the telltale sound of his wings cutting through the air. It was completely and utterly silent. She slowed, looked around and saw that everything around her had changed. The morning sun didn't shine here. It was twilight everywhere she looked and when she lifted her snout to sniff the air the only thing she was able to scent was the arcane.

Emmett's magic was everywhere. There was no escaping it. It didn't matter how fast she ran, she'd never reach the old witch's cabin.

"Stop running."

She wheeled around to see Emmett standing in all his terrible Fae glory. He was as naked as she was, wings unfurled behind him as he walked towards her. His eyes were pitch black, and the closer he came to her the heavier twilight settled around them. Birdie backed away from him. Just because she knew she wasn't going to reach Jazzy's cabin didn't mean she was going to give up. She moved to dash away from Emmett but she'd only taken a step when he stopped her.

"Shift," his command hit her like a mac truck and she screamed as her body obeyed. Her spine cracked, her claws vanished in an instant, and she fell to the ground on her hands and knees. She knew the Fae had control over shifters. Their particular sway of magic was so intertwined in the creation of shifters that it was both sacred and reviled in their worlds. To be a Fae's mate was no easy thing and somehow it was Birdie's burden to bear.

"That was a real dick move," she gritted out between clenched teeth. She looked over her shoulder at him. "Get away from me."

"You shouldn't run from me."

She pushed herself up from the ground and took a step away from him. "Funny. That seems to be all I want to do right now," she told him. Birdie turned, running as fast as she was able to on her tired limbs. Shifting took it out of her, made her ache from the exertion, but she refused to submit to Emmett. Her decision to run was more for herself than anything. She knew he'd catch her, but she ran anyway. Because it was *her* choice to. That's what this was all about anyway.

Emmett pinned her to the ground. "Where do you think you're going, beloved?" he growled in her ear.

"Get off!" Birdie bucked her hips trying to get him off, but the only thing it did was bring her body flush to his. She bit her lip and tried to hold back the moan of pleasure it brought her to be this close to him. She swung her fist and it glanced off his shoulder, she pushed him away from her.

"Let me go!"

Emmett took the hits and pushes from Birdie without flinching. He held her tight even while she struggled against him. "I'm never going to do that. You're mine, Birdie. You know this." He stared down at her with black eyes.

"It's not fair!" she screamed up at him.

Emmett didn't let her go and for all the force of keeping her in place, his touch was not rough. It was gentle, unmoving as the mountains around them, but that was the extent of his hold on her. He moved her hands, collaring her wrists in one of his hands as he leaned over her.

"What's not fair?" he asked her.

She glared up at him. The ground was soft beneath her, a bed of moss that felt better than her mattress at home. It was the work of Emmett's magic. Even now he was seeing to her comfort.

"This. *All of this.* You weren't supposed to reject me."

"I know, beloved."

"You didn't choose me, and-and I want to choose, too. That's why I went to your grandmother," she told him. The words were coming faster now, the ones she'd kept hidden from Rosie, kept them away from even herself, because she'd been terrified if she gave voice to them they'd overtake her.

"I want to choose too. You got to and it's not fair I have to be the one trying to keep from drowning. I don't know if you'll wake up and decide you don't want me again. Do you think I can take that? *I can't!* And I don't want to be this scared!" Her voice cracked on the last word.

Scared.

That was the word she'd tried to stay away from, because it was the truth of it all. She was scared shitless. Her shoulders shook as hot tears spilled down her cheeks. She was so damn scared, because she knew what they could be. What they should have been from the start. She knew he could claim her now. That she couldn't stop him if he decided to. *Luna.* She knew she shouldn't take comfort in knowing that even if she did not choose it, it was within his power to make it so but even still...the choice of it all was the thing she craved.

Emmett's eyes went gray and his wings vanished. He was the man she'd seen that first moment in the library, the one she'd tried to give herself to at the first sign of their mate bond. He shook his head and cupped her face.

"Beloved, I'm so fucking sorry," he whispered to her. He kissed her cheek and let her wrists go to wipe her tears away with featherlight touches. "I'm sorry, Birdie. I'm sorry." She knew he was. That he wasn't lying to her. The bond between them was golden in the twilight, lighting them up despite the gloom all around them. There was no getting rid of it. Not now. Not ever.

She hiccuped and nodded. "I know."

For better or worse. This was her mate. Her fate was tied to his in the way that one moment was never just hers or his. It belonged to them both. Just like the rest of their days would be.

"I will choose you. *Over and over again*. And if you never trust me enough to choose me, I'll endure it."

She shook her head. "Please don't say that."

"I mean it. Even if you never give me your heart, I will wait for you, Birdie Salazar. I won't claim you until you ask me. You decide when, beloved."

Birdie's heart cracked. The fear and doubt she'd let pour out of her was washed away with those words. He meant it. Emmett, both the man and the Fae, was hers to take or leave as she saw fit. But he was hers all the same.

It was all she'd wanted from him.

"It's yours," she whispered.

"What?" He moved close, a look of awe on his face that made her heart stutter.

"It's yours," she told him again, her voice a little louder as she repeated it. She would say it a thousand times over just to keep that look on his beautiful face. She reached up and cupped his cheek in her hand. "My heart, I mean. It's yours."

"Birdie," he husked out, "my sweet mate. Beloved." He kissed her. It was slow and gentle, the slide of his mouth against hers made her sigh with pleasure.

"Birdie," he said again against her lips.

"I want you." She kissed him, wrapped her arms around him and held on like she'd ached to do from the very start. "I want you, Emmett. I-I," her voice stuttered and she found it, the words she'd been trying to hide from came to her easily now, "Claim me."

Emmett sucked in a breath and the awe turned to wonder as he looked her over. "I don't have to. Not if it-"

She moved up and claimed his mouth. She kissed him hard and then broke the kiss to move to his shoulder. The space that met his neck. She nipped at it, not enough to break the skin, but enough to promise what would come. This was the place their mate bond would be sealed. This was the place the claiming mark would take the best. She grinned when she heard the low rumble of a growl in his chest.

"You will be mine in every way after I have you," he warned her. "No escaping me. No running from me."

"I know." She lay back on the bed of moss and stared up at her mate. "I want it. I want to be yours. Please, I-"

He cut off her words with a rough kiss. "Please is

not something you say to me. Ask it. Demand it of me and it will be yours."

She smiled and kissed him. He wanted her to be greedy with him. She could do that. She raised a leg and wrapped it around his hip as she pulled him towards her. The feel of his muscled body beneath her hands, above her as he moved closer to her and settled between her thighs, set her body alight with pleasure. She dug her nails into his shoulders and pulled him closer.

"I want you inside of me."

Emmett groaned, head falling forward so that his lips were against her ear. "You are more than I could have ever wished for." The head of his cock nudged at her entrance and Birdie sucked a breath in when he moved a hand between them. He gripped his cock and moved it, dragged it through her wet folds, coated himself in her cream as he teased her.

"Emmett," she groaned and lifted her hips to meet the next slide of his cock, to take the head of him into her with a sigh of pleasure. It was ecstasy already and he'd only given her an inch. "More, I need more."

He moved, hips thrusting forward as he sank another inch into her with a groan. "You are so beauti-ful. My perfect mate," he whispered, lips brushing the shell of her ear as he fed her his length. Birdie cried out when he moved again. The stretch of Emmett's cock inside of her walked the line of pain and pleasure. All of it mixed up in the beautifully imperfect way that left her hungry for more. She raised her hips and met his next thrust, taking him fully into her.

"Beloved," he sighed against her neck. He kissed the column of her neck, peppered her skin with kisses as he began to move. Birdie wrapped her legs around him, pulling him deeper inside of her. Emmett held her tightly, the roll of hips taking on an extra punch as he claimed her. It didn't take long for Birdie to find her release. Her body shook, pussy squeezing his cock as she came, yet Emmett didn't stop. The edges of her orgasm softened and turned into the next as her mate fucked her through her orgasm and into the next.

He groaned and Birdie looked up at him. He was watching her with that same hungry look he'd had when he'd seen her at the auction and again in the bar. The same as when he chased her down.

She had to have him. Had to have her mate once and for all. She reached for him, hands pulling him down to her so that his neck was against her lips.

"Do it," he groaned, hands coming to either side of her as he held himself still for her.

Birdie didn't hesitate. She sank her teeth into his neck and claimed him like her body and heart demanded she do. Emmett moaned at her bite and satisfaction that hit her, left her breathless and trembling. This was right. It had always been right. Why had she run from it? He was hers and she was his. That was the way it was meant to be...except, that she wasn't *quite* his.

Not yet.

But she would be. Birdie moved her head, angled her neck to him, offering it up to his claiming bite. Emmett let out a ragged chuckle and his breath ghosted over her skin as he groaned.

"Oh yes." He sank his teeth into her neck and Birdie screamed, the sound of it muffled against his shoulder as she came once more on her mate's cock.

Afterwards, he held her close. He kissed her every place he was able, touched her reverently and whispered promises of their future to her. Birdie reveled in it. There was no fear or doubt, only hope and the kind of peace that came with utter certainty and knowing. Because there were three things Birdie knew when it came to her Fae mate.

They were one and the same.
They were bonded now and forever.
They were now the way they should have been from the start.

EPILOGUE

"**I** really don't think you should be pissy at your grandma, okay?" Birdie arranged the flowers she was carrying in her arms and squinted up at the cabin.

"Oh, I'm plenty of things at her, but being pissy isn't one of them. Try irate, furious, or incensed," Emmett told her with a scowl.

"Those are all just synonyms for pissy," she pointed out. Emmett frowned but said nothing, because she was right. She'd been picking up a lot of handy dandy facts like that from her word of the day calendar she'd gotten on a whim last month.

She grinned at him and poked him in the side. "She didn't mean any harm by it. You know that, right? She was just trying to help."

Emmett sighed and nodded at her. He wrapped an arm around her as they walked. They were in front of

Jazzy's cabin now. It was early October and leaves crunched underfoot. There had been snow, but only a light dusting was present now. Birdie knew a big storm was coming soon and had suggested they check in on his grandmother before it came. She hadn't seen the witch in the weeks that had followed her and Emmett's bonding but she figured it was long past due, really.

She knew the reason they hadn't been was because Emmett was still angry at her for meddling, but it was his fault she'd even been involved. Birdie had pointed this out when they were moving her things into his house a few days ago. She'd moved in pretty much the day they'd walked out of the forest together, their bond marks fresh on the other's neck, but she'd held on to her apartment a little longer. Though she'd given in when Emmett pointed out that it would be easier for her to get ready in the mornings if she was in possession of her full closet. Though, she suspected he did so because she kept stealing his fancy dress shirts to use because she didn't have a top and was already running late for her shift at the bar.

"Do you not like seeing me in your shirts?" she asked him, tying the dress shirt up into a half shirt with a knot.

He laughed and gathered her in his arms. "You can have all of them. I'll just buy more. I think I'd like seeing your things with mine, though. I want my scent all over your things, not just the things you forget here."

She'd liked that. Plus, Emmett had a great fireplace

in his house. She really loved that fireplace, so she'd moved in officially. This was their first weekend together and she was glad she'd forced him to come to see his grandmother.

"I know," he sighed and kissed the top of her head. "But she has a way of sticking her fingers in places they shouldn't be." He turned to look around the clearing and then the cabin. "And I smell her magic. She's been meddling again."

"Meddling? What do you mean?" Birdie asked. Now that he pointed it out she could pick up the sharp tang of magic. She was so used to Emmett's magic that she hadn't realized it, but where his felt warmer, smelled richer to her, this was stark and acrid. It burned her nose when she inhaled and she sneezed.

"Oh, shit, that's big magic."

He nodded. "It is. Come on."

They approached the cabin and climbed the stairs but didn't get any further before the door swung open and Jazzy marched out with a group of women behind her.

"And don't you give in as soon as he comes crying," she advised the women. "Can't let them off easy like my grandson here." She pointed a hand at Emmett and then smiled at Birdie. "Glad to see you again, dear."

"Hi, Jazzy."

"Grandmother. What have you done?"

Jazzy winked and passed a hanky to one of the women who was sniffling. She patted her shoulder with a shake of her head. "It's all right, dear. You'll see. I promise," she told the woman who nodded at her with a watery smile.

"Thank you for what you did. I couldn't take it anymore. None of us could."

Birdie's mouth dropped open because the pieces clicked right into place. She knew exactly what Jazzy had done and she clapped a hand over her mouth with a laugh.

"Hell yeah, Jazzy!"

"*Grandmother,*" Emmett sighed, and looked at the sky. "Please tell me you didn't..."

Jazzy huffed and threw her long silvery braid over her shoulder. "I did, and I'll tell you why I did. I'm tired of mates thinking they deserve better than they get. There's something wrong around here with this way of thinking and I'm not having it for one second more."

Emmett was silent for a moment. The women watched them and Birdie was painfully aware of how they zeroed in on the arm around her shoulder, the flowers that she carried in her arms.

"These are you for you," she said, holding them out to Jazzy, who beamed at her.

"Thank you, dear."

Birdie inclined her head and looked at the women. They had the same pained look she'd seen in herself. The same type of fear that would bring them to a Fae witch in the middle of nowhere, because there was no other way to find peace. She understood why they'd come here, because she'd done it, too.

Their pain mattered just as much as the peace they were looking for. Jazzy had been busy that afternoon, judging from the half dozen women who stared back at Birdie. Each and every one of them had their mate bond cut out by the Fae witch, just like she had.

"I'm glad she did it for me, and it's going to be okay for you too. I swear."

BUCKLE UP, BUTTERCUP. I'M STARTING A NEW SERIES with the Red River Rejected Mates Series! Sign up for my newsletter to keep up with all my latest happenings and to know when the Red River fun goes down.

This is the book I wrote to get my mojo back. If you've ever felt burnt to a veritable crisp and uncertain where to go next, just know that was me when I got this idea for *Librarian and the Bear*.

A book, I might add, that I had thought up a year ago. Yes, a whole dang year but life has a funny way of slowing you down and making you learn lessons for your own good. Once I did, I was able to bang this baby out and it felt so damn good! If you've read my books since the beginning you know my style is continuously evolving. I'm so grateful to get pushed to new levels with each and every book I write. It's easy to do when you're absolutely convinced this is the best book, your most favorite book, that you've ever written.

Librarian and the Bear was so easy to feel that about. Birdie and Emmett were perfect for me in every way and I hope you loved another look at the world of Oak Fast. Plus, there's the fact that I started out as a fanfic writer and rejected soulmates and fated mates gone awry has ALWAYS BEEN MY JAM. My catnip of preference and one that is so very difficult to find that suits my tastes. That's why I decided to write this book +

launch a new series! I'm so happy to broaden the world I've built with Red River. Think of it as me adding a new territory to the game board of my little magical world. I'll come up with a map soon so you can see what what I mean.

Yes, a map. I am that geeked out and psyched about this world. I'm so grateful to have you along with me for this adventure! Thank you for reading and loving this book as much as I do, and I hope you come with me on a whole series of Rejected Mates angsty deliciousness.

Sign up for my newsletter to get updates on my WIPs, giveaways and more from me, baby! ***https://bit.ly/2YU7Ovf***

Reformed Bad Boy + Good Girl Romance

Once Bitten

Twice Shy COMING SOON!

Gold Sky Historical Series

Diverse 19th Century Historical Romance

Heart and Hand: Interracial Mail Order Bride Romance Gold Sky Series Book One

Hearth and Home: Interracial Mail Order Groom Romance Gold Sky Series Book Two

Honor and Desire: Friends to Lovers Gold Sky Series Book Three

Three to Love: A MMF Romance Gold Sky Series Book Four

Leather and Lace: A Lesbian Historical Novella Gold Sky Book Five

Pride and Passion : Enemies to Lovers Romance (Gold Sky Book 6)

Rose and Wicked: Marriage of Convenience (Gold Sky Book 7)

Stand Alone Romance Novels and Novellas

Auld Lang Syne: A Highlands Holiday Novella

Sugar and Spice: A Christmas Novella

Love And Gravity: A STEM Romance

ABOUT THE AUTHOR

Rebel Carter loves love. So much in fact that she decided to write the love stories she desperately wanted to read. A book by Rebel means diverse characters, sexy banter, a real big helping of steamy scenes, and, of course, a whole lotta heart. Rebel lives in Colorado, makes a mean espresso, and is hell-bent on filling your bookcase with as many romance stories as humanly possible!

Join my newsletter to know what the heck I'm doing next! ***https://bit.ly/2YU7Ovf***